Your Madness, Not Mine

Stories of Cameroon

by Makuchi

with an introduction by
Eloise A. Brière

Ohio University Center for International Studies
Monographs in International Studies
Africa Series No. 70
Athens

The books in the Center for International Studies Monograph Series
are printed on acid-free paper ∞™

03 02 01 00 99   5 4 3 2 1

Library of Congress Cataloging-in-Publication Data

Nfah-Abbenyi, Juliana Makuchi, 1958–
    Your madness, not mine : stories of Cameroon / by Makuchi ; with an
introduction by Eloise A. Brière.
        p.   cm. — (Monographs in international studies. Africa series ; no. 70)
    Includes bibliographical references.
    Contents: The healer — Your madness, not mine — Market scene — The
forest will claim you too — Election fever — American lottery — Accidents are
a sideshow — Bayam-sellam — Slow poison.
    ISBN 0-89680-206-x (alk. paper)
    1. Cameroon—Social life and customs—Fiction.   I. Ohio University. Center
for International Studies.   II. Title.   III. Series.
PR9372.9.N39Y68   1999   98-48353
823—dc21   CIP

For Ezekiel Takumberh Nfah

10 April 1965–26 December 1995

Contents

Mourning . . . in distant lands

Call me back in ten minutes
call me back
call me
ten minutes
ten
nine eight seven

CALL ME BACK
011 237 31 . . .
Hello
but, but, I only spoke with him
yesterday, this morning
WE talked about him
he was coming
HOME
next week, the doctors said.
New Year's at home, the doctors said.

How does one mourn?
How does one mourn in distant lands
holed up like a caged rat
hemmed in
barricaded behind cold friendless dreary cubic walls?

Day one
Day two

Day 3? Day 4? Day 5?
Sunrise? or sunset?
Mid-day? or mid-night?

voices echoing, bountiful
bouncing off the hole in my head
licking my face, teasing my eyes
Shadows
like wisps of smoke
swirling in the cave
gushing through skin consuming flesh
feeding the chimney.

The furnace that burnt within him
unnoticed
The furnace that churned and shredded his insides
sealed and safe, on the outside.

And the others
their charred bodies
he observed, like a film noir
their moans their groans their screams
their white-red-black-orange parched skins
items on his daily menu.

He ate with their sheets soaked in red-black mucus
He drank with their murmurs caressing him to sleep
take me, take me now . . .

Outside, the whiteness disappearing
Outside, blackness creeping home
stealthily
like darkness sweeping over his skin
And yet
the harmattan within raged,
nibbling away at the walls of the cave.

Face expanding, head exploding
skin stretched taut like a burn victim
i am afraid to touch
i am unable to numb the pain.

Heard about your brother, they say
Died in some sort of freakish accident?
Call me
if you want to talk
confined in my private jail
my ancestors, where are you?
when my tongue is tethered
when i am too weak to howl.

Are you mad?
You *don't ask*
you *come over*
you *sit with me*
you *hold my hand*
you *cuddle me*
you sing songs
we sing, we weep, we dance, we smile
we invoke them
And Taku reveals
he's at peace
how he loved life
how he almost cheated death
almost.

How does one mourn in distant lands?
eyes vapid like the Sahara
body drifting through bales of harmattan winds
punctured by a million needle heads.

No, it was no freakish accident
a natural gas explosion blew away our tongues
cloaking us in silence

of what is said
of what is heard and left unsaid
shredding my insides paper thin
my gaping wounds left exposed

blood satiating choking
day 6? day 7? day 8?
one week?

Ngiembuh, Afuba, Nkontemurh, Baba . . . Takumberh
I implore you, Oh, ancestors,
May you summon the early harmattan storm
To flood the desert within me.

Introduction

Eloise A. Brière

What does it mean to be a Cameroonian woman and to write in English? Makuchi is a Beba woman from Cameroon in Central Africa. She writes in English: not the King's English, not Gandhi's English nor Uncle Sam's English. What is it like, writing in English in a former British colony? Is that experience like putting on a straitjacket bequeathed to the Beba by the British colonizers of West Cameroon? Is the continuing use of Western languages as well as Western standards, religious beliefs, and technologies in former colonies such as Cameroon a measure of the success of colonization? Has the unique Beba perspective on the world been forever silenced by the global postcolonial interests whose watchdog agencies speak for Cameroonians, using the abstract universalist language that inevitably disfigures and shortchanges those they describe?

The short stories in this collection by Makuchi are a foil to such disfigurement. The reader will find no abstract universalist terms here, none of the language one finds in reports on Cameroon by United Nations commissions or the International Monetary Fund. These portraits of Cameroonians bring the reader directly into the heart of the postcolonial world, into the hearts of people. Makuchi's characters, like all

Cameroonians, have been left to deal with colonization's remnants and the ever-present neocolonial umbilical cord that connects Cameroon to both of its former colonizers, England and France. The characters Makuchi creates are survivors; they are scrappy and they are strong, especially the women. As we enter their world and see the neocolonial forces of gargantuan proportions that shape their daily living, Makuchi's pen guides us into a new literary space. She wields her pen like a pioneer's axe in the forest, clearing new spaces in literary discourse that invite us to consider realities we would otherwise never know. And as we read, Makuchi uproots her people from silence and transplants them into new soil, staking out new possibilities for growth, for expression.

It is now nearly forty years since Cameroon gained independence from France and England and many more years since the departure of Germany, the first European power to colonize Cameroon.[1] When representatives of the major European nations, the United States, and the Ottoman Empire gathered around a conference table in Berlin at the end of the nineteenth century to facilitate European penetration of West Africa, there had not yet been time for Africa to recover—if ever she could—from the loss of millions who had been enslaved and taken to the New World.[2] Now the pact signed at the 1885 Conference of Berlin would signal yet another major disruption for the continent: colonization.[3] Colonial empires built on the African continent by Western powers, propelled by their hunger for raw materials and new markets for their manufactured goods, would shatter the fragile balance between humans and the environment fundamental to the survival of small cultures that characterized much of the continent's social organization for thousands of years.

Makuchi's stories are written in English for the simple reason that the Western part of Cameroon came under British jurisdiction after World War I.[4] Before the relatively late implantation of (mainly mission) schools in the British Cameroons, the verbal arts of Makuchi's Beba people were expressed in the Beba language. The spread of Euro-literature and the growth of literacy displaced local oral traditions. The tales, riddles, and legends that had nourished generations were displaced by Chaucer and Shakespeare taught by Europeans like the nuns at Our Lady of Lourdes Secondary School in Bamenda. Makuchi's encounter with Euro-literature at Our Lady of Lourdes would never have occurred had it not been for her mother's vision. Makuchi's mother did not know what kind of world awaited her daughter, but she did know it would be nothing like her own simple farming existence. She knew this new world would require literacy, education, and knowledge of Western ways. So she coaxed even more crops from the land to feed her sons and daughters so that her husband's mission school salary could be used to pay boarding school fees for the children. At boarding school, later at Cameroon's flagship university at Yaoundé, and finally at McGill University in Montreal, Canada, Makuchi became the scholar her mother somehow knew she would be. Not content with a doctorate in African Literatures, Makuchi later earned a Ph.D. in Comparative Literature at McGill, the first Beba woman to earn two doctorates.

Cameroon is the only African country to have two European official languages, in contrast with most other African countries where either French or English, but not both, became the official language at independence.[5] There is, however, an imbalance between French and English in Cameroon due to population size and French postcolonial cultural policy. The English-speaking part of the country, which has only one-quarter of the population, does not face the same pressures from its former colonizer as does its French-speaking counterpart from France. Since Cameroon's independence in 1960, France has been extensively involved in continuing to promote its own culture and education system in francophone Cameroon.[6] Nowhere is French advocacy more evident than at the University of Yaoundé in Cameroon's capital. Bilingual in theory, it was conceived as a place where every student would be able to take any course in either English or French, yet the balance between the two languages weighs heavily in favor of French. As a result, it is the students from West Cameroon, like Makuchi, who become bilingual.[7] In the process they discover what it means to be part of a minority in their own country.[8] They learn that the word "anglophone" has become an insult, used by many, like the shopkeeper in the short story "Market Scene," as the derogatory equivalent of "foreigner" ("tu dois être anglophone . . . Pars, anglose . . . go! go witti your baluck, anglose!"). Little wonder then that in the 1980s students naturally gravitated toward the small English-language intellectual community that was emerging in the capital.[9]

Cameroon's literature in French was launched essentially after World War II in France, where young writers such as Mongo Beti and Ferdinand Oyono wrote anticolonial novels during their student years. Cameroon's anglophone literature was also launched abroad, but in the neighboring British colony of Nigeria, where writers such as Sankie Maimo and Vincent Nchami wrote works that reflected the clash of cultures produced by colonization. As she studied African literatures at the University of Yaoundé, Makuchi perfected her French, encountering few anglophone writers and fewer still women writers in her course of study.[10] While francophone writers had access to one of Africa's first publishing houses, Editions CLE in Yaoundé, little was available for anglophones.[11] Anglophone professors like Bole Butake encouraged budding anglophone writers by founding the student publication *The Mould: A Magazine of Creative Writing*, published by the Department of English at Yaoundé.[12] It was there that Makuchi got her start, publishing a short story in the third issue.[13] However, during her student years the creative writer would take a back seat to the scholar as Makuchi embarked on a project as part of her graduation requirements for the doctorate. Thanks to her research, the Beba oral tradition has been recorded for the first time.[14]

In *Your Madness, Not Mine*, Makuchi's language is that of Cameroonians—those who are unseen and unheard in official reports, those whose daily lives are reflected in the way they speak. Most Cameroonians speak three or more languages; multilingualism is a fact of daily life. Thus it is simply impossible for Makuchi to create characters that are monolingual.[15] Those who live in the anglophone provinces also use a Pidgin that originally arose in Cameroon to fill the linguistic vacuum that existed between English-speaking Europeans and Africans who spoke their own languages. Its use was limited mainly to trade in precolonial times; since then it has grown in complexity and usefulness.[16] Today it is the vehicle for songs, witticisms, orature, liturgical writings, and sermons and is the most frequently heard language in some parts of Cameroon.[17] When anglophone Cameroonians come to live in Yaoundé, they bring Pidgin, English, and their mother tongues to the linguistic mix in the capital city. In turn they add bits and pieces of French to their own linguistic repertoire. As one of the women in "Market Scene" says, "we had all come a long way from home, we were all in the business of survival." The linguistic mix spoken by Cameroonians in the capital is indeed the language of survival, the language of rural depopulation. Like Sibora's children in "Market Scene," who speak their mother tongue at home, Pidgin with their neighbor, and French—the school language—among themselves, Cameroonians share in the complex linguistic reality of the postcolonial world. Monolingualism is a luxury few can afford in a world where survival requires more than one language. Makuchi is one of the first African writers to not only allow us to hear the rich linguistic mosaic that characterizes modern Africa, but to also show us how language, class, and power intersect in the postcolonial context.

In *Your Madness, Not Mine,* Western economic interests are far from abstract as we see how lives are deeply affected by decisions made in the boardrooms of Paris, London, or New York. French and Asian logging interests destroy Cameroon's primeval forests in "The Forest Will Claim You Too"—tugging at its social fabric, tearing it as loggers overturn the delicate balance between man and nature. Tearing it so that healers can no longer find the ingredients the forest once provided for their medicines. Tearing it as young women bear "timber babies" fathered by the temporary workers brought in to clear the land. Like the deep marks left on the natural and human order by logging interests, so too does the urban landscape bear the scars of Western economic and cultural dumping. Billboards of the Marlboro Man in "American Lottery" invite passersby into the American dream even as Americans are forsaking tobacco. In Yaoundé, the capital, the lilt of local Bantu languages is scorned for the more progressive-sounding names like Santa Barbara or Dallas. The naming of new neighborhoods for such old U.S. television series reflects the plight of third world television broadcasting, which relies on hand-me-downs because they are the most affordable.

The attraction of the United States comes not so much from the pull of the Marlboro Man, the wealthy Texans of *Dallas,* or other U.S. cultural icons, as it does from the sharp economic decline in Cameroon. The 1990s contrast markedly with the economic boom times of the seventies and eighties, when Cameroon was Africa's success story. Economically crushed in the 1990s, professionals found their incomes reduced by more than half after the devaluation of Cameroon's currency (CFA) and other measures. It was not surprising that Cameroon's intellectual elite should join the African brain drain currently enjoyed by the United States. Free from the strong attachment to France that characterizes francophone Cameroonians and resentful of the linguistic discrimination they often experienced at home, anglophone Cameroonians were the first to join this exodus. "American Lottery" shows the tremendous pull exerted by the hope for a better life; it also shows an American reality that bears little resemblance to the carefree ways of the Marlboro Man. Coming to the United States means becoming invisible, being defined by a single characteristic—skin color—rather than the complex mass of traits that constitute a person in the Cameroonian context. Coming to the United States means living a symbolic death as the ties to the extended family become more tenuous, expressed only through telephone and internet links. As we see in the liminal poem "Mourning . . . in distant lands," such links serve only to increase the feelings of isolation. Technology does not nurture the African immigrant, nor do the daily encounters with American individualism and racism. Even as the material signs of success accrue to the African immigrant, daily life in the United States is lived as a form of impoverishment.

For many of the characters in *Your Madness, Not Mine*, education is the key to change. Lack of it can mean not only a life of hardship, it can lead to death, as we see in "Slow Poison." In this story ignorance spurs the AIDS epidemic, finding fertile ground in practices and beliefs like the assumption that fat women are free from HIV. The illness destroys not only individuals but society as a whole. The common practice of shunning the infected breaks the ties that normally bind the African family. Education is not, however, a means to the restoration of broken social ties, particularly where women are concerned. The modern educated woman in the story "Your Madness, Not Mine" lacks the autonomy of the simple market trader Mi Ngiembuh in "Bayam-Sellam." While for her the only escape from the powerlessness of modern marriage is succumbing to rage, the more traditional Mi Ngiembuh finds self-realization—marriage or no marriage. Using the solidarity between market women, she creates a trading empire. The state must eventually bow to the resistance of the women in Makuchi's story, when the devaluation of the CFA franc threatens Mi Ngiembuh's business. The plucky leader of the market women knows how to respond to that threat.[18] Under her guidance, the women strike, bringing trade to a halt and causing the government to declare a state of emergency. Their strength derives from the twin pillars that support women's action: the sacred nature of their work in the production of both life and food.[19] While women's agency was a force to be reckoned with by British colonial administrators, today it is often no match for the pressures emanating from the West.[20] The traditional seat of women's power is hard-pressed to effectively resist the external forces that are shaping and transforming Cameroon. Like traditional women everywhere, the old woman in "The Forest Will Claim You Too" is reduced to powerlessness by her country's neocolonial economic relationship with the West.

Traditional women's agency is not always thwarted nor is it collective, as illustrated by the crafty grandmother in "Election Fever," quietly helping herself to the "pork" politicians dish out in the weeks before elections, giving her granddaughter a lesson in the use of politics. "The Healer," on the other hand, shows the extent to which women lack agency when faced with childlessness, a situation that can spell disaster for many women, but which has much greater social significance for African women. Childlessness can suggest such women bear a curse and that they are society's deadwood. The prospect of having no descendants is frightening because it means that there will not be the "social security" children normally provide for parents. More frightening still is the prospect of having no afterlife, for who will properly bury the childless and keep their memory alive, as only offspring can do? Such deep-seated fears are fertile territory for charlatans, such as Azembe in "The Healer," who claim to use traditional "remedies" to heal infertility.

The range of Western impact on Cameroonian life, from language to religion and economy, would seem to indicate that colonization has indeed been successful in this Central African country. If colonization was successful for the West, was it so for the rest of the world's nontechnologically based cultures? One must not be too quick to declare victory because if Makuchi is able to write as she does, then there is a place for counterhegemonic perspectives. There is a way for a different consciousness to assert itself and make its way in the world. Perhaps this is the consciousness that will begin to loosen the stranglehold the West has on the rest of the world. Whatever the outcome, it is singularly healthy that Makuchi knows that the madness the West has spread around the globe is in no way hers.

Notes

1. After Germany lost its colonies in World War I, Cameroon was divided in two, with England taking over West Cameroon, along the border of Britain's Nigerian colony, and France getting East Cameroon, a much larger territory.

2. Figures vary, but between six and fourteen million Africans were captured, enslaved, and—for those who survived the horrors of the slave ships—brought to the Americas to provide the labor for the development of the new lands that Europe had claimed for herself. As Africans working on the plantations in the Americas produced wealth for Europe, Africa was robbed of the possibility of economic self-sufficiency. The Berlin West Africa Conference took place a scant thirty-six years after France abolished slavery, following England's abolition of the slave trade in 1807. Slavery would continue in Brazil until 1888.

3. German Chancellor Otto von Bismark presided over the Conference of Berlin, 1884–85. The objective was for Europe to take steps to implant "progress, commerce and civilization" in Africa. This prepared the way for the carving up of Africa among European powers, who later signed bilateral accords respecting each other's rights to specific geographic areas.

4. Cameroon is made up of ten provinces; its two English-speaking provinces are in the west, the other eight are French-speaking.

5. See "Language and Language Policy in Cameroon" by Beban Sammy Chumbow in Ndiva Kofele-Kale, *An African Experiment in Nation Building: The Bilingual Cameroon Republic since Reunification* (Boulder, Colo.: Westview Press, 1980), 281–312.

6. France's involvement in almost all her former colonies extends far beyond the cultural. It is not unusual to find French advisors at key points in many governments, nor is it unusual for French businesses to have a quasi-monopoly in certain areas. For instance, in francophone Cameroon all textbooks are imported from France. French troops have never left the continent and are only a phone call away, should any of France's African "friends" be in a difficult situation. The currency is still the CFA franc, which was used in colonial times. While in French territories such as Martinique the CFA has been replaced by the French franc, the CFA franc is still in use in central and West Africa. In 1994 the French devalued the CFA franc, with dramatic repercussions all over West Africa. France maintains a coalition of over forty French-speaking countries worldwide through what is called La Francophonie, supported by an aid agency, Agence de Cooperation Culturelle et Technique, created in the twilight years of France's colonial empire.

7. "For many years, the number of lecturers [using] . . . French at the University was superior to staff using . . . English . . . ; so that despite its constitutional bilingual status, the university was, for over a decade, essentially a French language university." In a response to the need for bilinguals, "a special bilingual degree programme was introduced in the Faculty of Arts" (Chumbow, 292–93).

8. The Cameroonian constitution was recently modified, officially recognizing minorities and their special needs.

9. Dr. Bernard Fonlon contributed greatly to the creation of this community. Fonlon, who received university degrees in Ireland and England as well as at the Sorbonne, staunchly defended the merits of bilingualism when he was a government minister and later as head

of the Department of African Literatures at the University of Yaoundé. He shared his love of classical music through his Sunday afternoon radio program, which stimulated the postcolonial cultural climate in Cameroon, as did the journal he founded, *Abbia*, one of the first to be published in Africa. For many years this journal was a forum for both anglophone and francophone intellectuals. For a detailed examination of the anglophone-francophone situation in Cameroon, see Richard Bjornson, *The African Quest for Freedom and Identity: Cameroonian Writing and the National Experience.* (Bloomington: Indiana University Press, 1991), 278–310.

10. Although Marie Claire Matip published the novella *Ngonda* in 1954 (Yaoundé: Librairie "Au Messager") and Jeanne Ngo-Mai published her collection *Poèmes sauvages et lamentations* (Monte Carlo: Editions Regain) in 1967, the first full-length Cameroonian novel written by a woman, Thérèse Kuoh-Moukoury's *Rencontres essentielles* (Paris: Imprimerie Edgar) was not published until 1969. These works were not studied in university programs. Anglophone women writers began writing poetry and short stories while students at the University of Yaoundé in the 1980s. See Nalova Lyonga, "La littérature féminine anglophone au Cameroun," *Notre librairie* 118 (July–September 1994): 29–35, for a more complete discussion.

11. In an interview, Sankie Maimo, whose *Sov-Mbang: The Soothsayer, Drama* (1968) was the only anglophone work published by Cameroon's Editions CLE, complains that even though his works were published as early as 1959, they are not read (*Mould* 3 [May 1979]: 1–6). The lack of critical attention given to Maimo's work reflects the stranglehold of the French-trained intellectual elite on the reception of literature in Cameroon.

12. Today anglophone students have their own university, the University of Buea, which was founded in 1994. Creative writing continues to be fostered among students by Professor Nalova Lyonga, who encourages them to publish in *That Rocky Place*, a journal of creative writing about women that she publishes in the Department of English at the University of Buea.

13. "The Visiting Card" is a tragic story about the common practice of wealthy older married men who use high school students as prostitutes or mistresses. Makuchi's character, a high school boarding student, has a brief sexual encounter with an older man. She commits suicide after returning to her dormitory and reading the calling card the man has pressed into her hand: the man is her father.

14. Makuchi has made a significant contribution to the debate surrounding the place of gender in writing by African women. She places it in a pan-African context and argues that it is possible to develop an indigenous African critical theory. See Nfah-Abbenyi, Juliana Makuchi, *Gender in African Women's Writing: Identity, Sexuality, and Difference* (Bloomington: Indiana University Press, 1997).

15. Readers will note that Makuchi writes in Cameroonian English, not that of the United States. Cameroonians have "naturalized" British English, changing it to fit their needs while retaining most spelling conventions.

16. Michael Kelly remarks, "A number of common grammatical features distinguish English-based pidgins from English. For example plurals are marked differently (e.g. 'dem' is added behind the singular form of the noun) or are unmarked as they are implicit in the context: 'plenti man no get woman'. Genders may be marked by appropriate adding of man/woman: 'woman fowl; man pikin' (female hen, male child)." (Kelly, "Taking Pidgin Seriously," *Abbia: Revue culturelle camerounaise/Cameroon Cultural Review* 31–33 [February 1978]: 287).

17. For a discussion of Cameroonian Pidgin, see Loreto Todd, *Pidgins and Creoles* (London: Routledge and Kegan Paul, 1974).

18. See remarks on the CFA in note 6.

19. Women produce virtually all food crops in Cameroon, not only to feed their families but also to supply urban centers. The children they produce provide prestige and social standing. These two modes of production are the pillars of their power, the grounding that characterizes Makuchi's strong women. For a discussion of women's work in West Cameroon see Miriam Goheen, *Men Own Fields, Women Own the Crops: Gender and Power in the Cameroon Grassfield* (Madison: University of Wisconsin Press, 1996).

20. In "Riot and Rebellion among African Women: Three Examples of Women's Political Clout," Audrey Wipper describes the "Anlu Rebellion," in which seven thousand women in Western Cameroon revamped a traditional organization into a well-disciplined, powerful force for change, staging a series of mass demonstrations that led to their seizing control of tribal affairs (in *Perspectives on Power*, edited by Jean F. O'Barr [Durham, N.C.: Duke University Press, 1982], 50–72).

1

The Healer

When my uncle and I arrived at the compound, we were stunned by the chaos that stared us in the face. The entire compound looked ravaged, as if a troop of elephants had just passed through for breakfast. My uncle later said that what we saw had reminded him of the year when, as a young boy, the locusts had invaded our village. Following the coming of these "leeches-with-wings" (my uncle has a way with words), had the people not been protected by their ancestors, who had pleaded on their behalf to appease the village gods, they would all have died of starvation. The locusts had picked their crops bare of all their leaves. The devastation could be seen throughout the vast expanse of hills and valleys. But the gods had been kind to the people, for in their timely benevolence, they had unleashed the rainfall that had helped revive some of the plants. That was how they had been able to survive the-year-of-the-leeches-with-wings.

The compound we had just walked into, which was once bustling with life, looked desolate; there was pandemonium everywhere. The houses, the huts, everything: the whole compound had been burnt to ashes. Trickles of smoke could be seen rising from some of the mounds of earth. Men, women, children were scurrying around like incubating hens that hurriedly search for food before rushing back to nestle their eggs. Voices could be heard everywhere. The forest around was very much alive. The noise sounded like the din you normally hear only in our open-air village markets (as opposed to city markets where city folk are much too civilised to scream at the top of their heads for hours). We could hear relatives calling out to their loved ones, pushing through the crowds, hoping to find them before they bolted off into the forest, like some already had. I was appalled by the look on the faces of the "mental cases." Some of them were sitting on the ground, apparently not aware of what was happening. Some were picking up earth and rubbing it on their bodies, decorating themselves, making patterns as if they were building huts. Some were scavenging for food in the debris. I did not have time to think or observe all that was going on. My uncle and I were pushing through throngs of people, shouting my aunt's name at the top of our voices.

I spotted her, leaning against a tree, a young sapling that could barely hold her weight. I shouted her name and broke into a run, my uncle close behind me. I embraced her but she did not respond to my touch. She did not gather me in her arms as she was wont to do. My hands dropped to my sides as I looked up into her face. I could not believe that this woman staring at me as if I were an imperceptible evening shadow was my beloved aunt. I might as well have been staring at a total stranger (or rather, she must have taken me for a total stranger). I kept on scrutinising her face, inspecting the lines for those signs that only I knew. Not a single twitch of a muscle. I felt as if my eyes were drilling holes through her body, through her head—no, through her eyes. There were no shadows. I was hoping to recognise those shadows that only I saw.

But there was nothing. It was empty, totally empty—nothing. All I remember now are the tears, hot little streams rolling down my cheeks as my uncle gently took my aunt in his arms and led the way back home. It would take her six months to tell me (in confidence) what had happened that day. Till today, I still think that what she told me barely scratched the surface of the whole story, a story that no one will ever know in its entirety, for only one person knew and could tell the stories, but he is no condition or position to do so. Even if he were alive, he would never have told; he would have carried most of those stories to his grave.

Azembe's compound was strategically situated just beyond the outskirts of Yaoundé. No one could drive up to this compound. Not that there was no road. There was. The procedure was simple. You had to take the tarred road to the outskirts of the town, get off this main road, and drive another five kilometres on a well-paved laterite road until you got to the junction that led to his compound. The road meandered on, but at this junction you had to get off the car and walk another kilometre on foot. At one point, the road seemed simply to disappear and merge into a path. You then had to take this path and trek through the dense equatorial forest, hastening your step, trying hard not to look up into those tall trees, when suddenly you arrived at an open space. The sensation you felt was one of an animal caught and blinded in the deep of the night by the light of a hunter's burning torch.

Azembe's compound looked like a small village that had been uprooted from somewhere and planted here, in this clearing, right in the middle of the forest. It consisted of two big houses facing each other (one in which he received his patients and visitors, and the other in which he kept countless medicines and did his magic on the frail bodies of suffering humans). These two imposing houses were surrounded by a conglomerate of little thatched huts. In these, his patients spent their nights and days, languishing in their pain or taking comfort from the relatives who helped them nurse themselves back to normal, healthy lives.

Azembe was renowned all over the land. His name was on the lips of many people because it was claimed that he would succeed where every other man had failed. He was therefore the last step to survival, his compound the point of no return. You either left that little clearing in the forest dead or alive. Such was his power of healing. He brought the dead back to life, they said. He could go into the depths of other worlds, imbibe with evil spirits, fight them, beat them, and snatch the lives of his patients back just as their souls were being wrenched away from them. He spoke the language of the living dead like few mortals could. His power had become legendary. It is said that his late father, who had learned his craft from his late mother (that woman of whom it was said that her witchery was too pregnant for a single being to nurture and engender), had been known to take his son on those journeys deep into the woods, deep into the world of the living dead, when Azembe was still in his mother's womb. It was said that on such nights his mother would lie on her bed and feel as if the life was being sucked out of her. She would lie there on her bamboo bed, exhausted, almost dead but for her breathing, until her husband returned with her son. She had been the first to know that Azembe had been the chosen one and had raised him differently from the day he was born.

Azembe had not disappointed his ancestors. He had excelled in his craft, so much so that it was said that if Cameroon chose to go to war with any of her neighbours—Chad, Gabon, Equatorial Guinea, the Central African Republic, or Nigeria, especially Nigeria (Cameroonians claimed that the others were chicken feed)—all the government had to do was prostrate itself in front of Azembe, and he would walk (of course, nobody would see him) ahead of the army and harvest the bullets and shells from those Nigerian guns and cannons. It was as simple as that. The Cameroonian army would only have to march on behind him, or rather they would have to imagine and keep a respectful distance. The Nigerian soldiers would have fled from what they saw and could not see, what they knew but could not know, and the Cameroonians would declare victory.

Yes, Azembe had become a legend in his own lifetime. Why am I telling you about this man, you might be asking yourself? It is because my aunt, like hundreds of women, had travelled hundreds of kilometres to consult this powerful healer. She could not have children. You know what they say about women who cannot have children. My aunt (the one that I love dearly) told me that she knew she had neither been cursed by her ancestors nor by her marriage (her husband's paternal grandmother, to be exact), as some diviners had claimed. She simply felt that her womb was not the hurrying type (whatever she meant by that). She said her womb was taking its time; it was a late bloomer that needed more time to be coaxed into nurturing the special child that she was going to have. She even claimed that this special one would one day rule the world. I loved my aunt even more when she told me these delightful stories about her very special children who were still refusing to come into the world. I longed to hold one of these unique cousins in my arms. Lord knows, I have held many children. When you grow up like I did, with many brothers, sisters, cousins, nephews, and nieces, you take care of babies whether you like it or not. You baby-sit your siblings and relatives. You partake in raising them. It is your duty to them and to the family. You learn to raise others and they learn to raise others as well. My grandmother says that that is what keeps the chain going. It must never be broken.

I have never known what it feels like to hold a special child in one's arms, so I longed to hold my aunt's special child. People have dreams of becoming president or minister; I dreamed of my aunt's child. Looking back, I think my aunt was at the root of this dream. Ordinarily, she is a very happy, vivacious, outgoing woman. I have admired the fact that she always said what came to her mind first, and only thought about it later. My mother often referred to her sister as the-one-who-cannot-hold-her-tongue. True, she had a sharp tongue, but she rarely said anything in malice. If she had anything spiteful to say about you, she said it to your face. For that reason, few bore her grudges (except the jealous ones). But my aunt's cheerfulness was marred by something, something that lay hidden somewhere behind her eyeballs (I do not know how else to describe it). When I saw that thing lingering furtively behind those limpid eyes, I knew she was sad. No matter how heartily she laughed, I never failed to see the little creases that formed at the tails of both those eyes when she was happy. Such thoughts made me even more determined to see this child who could erase the little lines at the tail of my aunt's eyes. So, I waited, she waited, we were waiting together. I don't know whether she knew that.

This trouble invaded our lives while I was living with my uncle, a civil servant working in Yaoundé. He had heard so much about Azembe that he had finally decided to take his sister to see the famed healer. My uncle claims that this was one of the most difficult and painful decisions he has had to make. You see, my uncle is what we call in the family the staunch Catholic and a well-educated man. He has often been heard dismissing these healers with a sweep of the hand. Charlatans, he calls them. Not that he did not have respect for traditional medicine. He did. He even revered some of the healers whom, he said, not only knew their roots, barks of trees, and potent leaves but also had a total grasp of the psychology of their patients, an acute understanding and respect for the philosophies that govern their daily existence within their families and environment. But my uncle also said that many of these self-proclaimed witch doctors, medicine men, ngambe men (diviners), sorcerers—the list goes on—were quacks. You had to be there to hear my uncle say the word *quack*. I don't think the British ever intended it to be said that way. They would have either loved to hear my uncle's phonetic expression or scoffed at him with a phrase like, "Listen to these upstarts (of the empire) dilute and adulterate the English language!" My uncle said this word—no, he spat it out like someone crushing a palm kernel or kola nut against their teeth. He said that what these people did was mere quackery, plain and simple. It was sheer exploitation. My uncle did not go into detail, but we had heard tangible rumours in our neighbourhood.

The police officer who lived four houses away from my uncle's had three wives. The second wife could not have children after she had the second child, so, they say, he married a third wife, who also did not have children the first three years of her marriage. The police officer had decided that it was time to see Azembe. He had the money, so cost was not a problem. He decided to kill two birds with one stone and sent his two wives to Azembe. The treatment went well. They both had children, one a boy, the other, a girl. But something curious, something devious, revealed itself as the two children got older. When they stared into each other's face, they seemed to reflect the same image, the same eyes staring into the same square face. The family had pretended to overlook the resemblance when the babies were younger, telling every visitor, "Ooooh, oooh! They look so much like their father." The visitors would believe them if they did not know the policeman. Had they known the officer, they would not see any resemblance between the square angular faces of these children and the svelte, bony face that was the policeman's. His was a long face, with scarification marks that gave him the look of the ancestral mask of an earth goddess. Those visitors who knew the truth, especially the women, admired the children, praised them, commented on how healthy they looked and reserved their laughter and mockery for when they were out of sight and earshot. The men usually mumbled a few polite words and sat down to drink the beer that was offered. My curiosity had not kept me from visiting this home to verify the story. I understood why it had taken my uncle the time that it did for him to finally make up his mind to take his beloved sister to Azembe. He must have seen those shadows that I see as well. I remember him mumbling something about my aunt's happiness being more important than his own feelings and convictions. If Azembe would help erase those shadows, then to Azembe's she had to go.

My aunt woke up that morning feeling weak and tired, almost dazed. It looked and felt as if she had slept all night. But it was past midday already, which meant she had slept a lot—far too much. My aunt was alarmed because she is an early riser. How could she have slept so much? She had never indulged herself like that before, and she never planned to. "Only lazy people or those fools who have no purpose in life do such things," she was wont to say. She tried to open her eyelids but they felt heavy as stone. She tried to lift herself from the bamboo bed, but her muscles ached, her joints ached, her whole body was on fire, so painful were the shooting little pains, like tiny arrows teasing her body to exhaustion. She felt like someone in a stupor, struggling to get over a hangover of cornbeer and palmwine. She told me that all she could recollect was that she had felt very drowsy after Azembe had given her her first treatment. The same thing had happened the following day. She had murmured that she felt drowsy, but Azembe had reassured her that it was the medication working and calmly advised her to go to sleep, "so that the medicine could do its job." Now she had slept a whole night and a whole day (my aunt said it was a whole day) and woke up with all these aches and pains that she could not explain. This medicine must be terrible, she had thought. "It is either very strong—god, it can kill someone—or it is useless and harmful. One or the other." That is my aunt. She often dismissed those things she could not personally explain as bad. That day went by, but the healer did not come to her hut. She had been hoping that Azembe would come to see her on his daily rounds and further explain why she felt so weak. But that was not to be. All she could remember was that she had slept the whole afternoon and only woke up a little before sunset, just as dusk was approaching. My aunt actually told me that she woke up at that graceful period of the day in Africa when shadows are as long as spiky ghosts, that period when chickens had already gone to roost, fast asleep, their heads neatly tucked under the warmth of their wings, enjoying dreams about worms and corn and grass and . . . Because she had to answer nature's call she had painfully dragged her aching limbs to the back of her hut. As she squatted to urinate, she felt something sticky, almost flaky, between her thighs. At first she ignored it and gladly went about the business of relieving a bladder that was full to capacity. As she dragged her feet back to her bamboo bed she felt something sticky trickle down and tickle her inner thighs as they rubbed themselves against each other, following the rhythm of her movement. She braced herself, entered the hut and sat down on her bed. With a gentle movement she lifted her right hand and touched and felt this liquid that was coming out of her body. She was alarmed. Her heart was racing, beating fast, faster than she had ever known. She was frightened as she began to imagine what might be happening to her. She wondered whether she was only hallucinating. But the smell at the tips of her fingers was unmistakable. It hit her nostrils like the smell of a hunter's urine that had been stored in a bottle or calabash for at least five days to make it more potent for the bush traps that lure in the game. Her nostrils contracted. She felt suffocated by the stench that suddenly engulfed her entire body, almost asphyxiating her.

Azembe did come to her hut the following evening, carrying the treatment with him. She told him that she needed to answer nature's call and promised to drink the medicine as soon as she returned. Azembe promised to come back and see how she was faring. He left her hut, and she emptied the contents of her treatment bowl under her bed. True to his word, he returned. My aunt was lying as still as night on her bamboo bed, pretending to be deep in sleep when Azembe made his stealthy entrance and tiptoed over to her bed. She felt his hand gently touch her forehead. Then she felt his hand gently raise her njagasa. Ever so lightly, she could feel her skirt being lifted inch after inch until it was gently placed on her stomach. She heard his loincloth drop like a feather and what happened next confirmed what she had dreaded all along.

My aunt looked me straight in the eye. There was an unexplainable sadness and emptiness in the deep waters that swirled around at the bottom of those eyes that I could not comprehend. It was at that precise moment, she said, that something had snapped in her head, invading her arteries, spreading through her entire body. The intense pain had miraculously evaporated and she seemed possessed, like her mother on those nights when granny donned her ancestral gear and went out to fight off those evil spirits that come to the village once in a while to steal the crops from our farms. No one could see, let alone recognise my grandmother when she was out on such missions. The rumbling sounds and cries through the hills told the people that she was out there taking care of business. They could sleep soundly and expect a good harvest.

My aunt, they said, had gone crazy. Had someone not heard Azembe's cry for help, she would have killed him with her bare hands, they said. Not only that, she had gone on a rampage of destruction and, like a wounded python thrashing through the hills, refusing to accept the moment of death, had systematically put fire to a number of huts. The thatched roofs had burned very fast, and the fire spread rapidly throughout the compound. People rushed to save themselves and their relatives. The police came too late. There was nothing left to salvage in this secluded village but hundreds of patients who looked scared, haggard, numb, not knowing where they were, not knowing where to go. So the police heard the stories told by many women who held their heads in shame.

Recently, I have noticed that the sparkle has begun to return, ever so fleetingly, to my aunt's eyes. That makes me very happy. But she told me the other day that there is one thing she cannot forgive. The stories of all those women were only worth a three-year prison sentence, one that Azembe did not even finish serving since it was claimed that he had died of a heart attack. You should have seen how tight my aunt pulled down the corners of her mouth and curled up her lips when she narrated this portion of the story. Not to mention the long line of spit that shot out of her mouth, making an endless arc that can stretch from here to nki mbu, the river that breeds tonnes of succulent mudfish.

2

Your Madness, Not Mine

"Do you want to play seven stones with me?" Beatrice asked her friend and neighbour Jikwu. She was juggling the stones in her right hand as she spoke. She proceeded to throw one stone after the other up in the air. The movements of her wrist and fingers were so well coordinated that it looked effortless as each stone left her right hand, made a semicircle in the air, and landed in her palm just as the next stone left its cradle. It looked magical, especially that none of the remaining stones, which seemed to be glued to her palm, fell to the ground. It was a masterful juggling act that she had perfected during her few years of growing up. Some children would drop a stone here, a stone there, but not Beatrice. Her stones just kept bouncing off each other, as if they all shared the same soul, as if responding to an extraterrestrial force and being. Beatrice managed to smile, all the while maintaining the rhythm of her play.

"Stop that!" Jikwu snapped.

"Why are you so irritated?"

"I said you should stop throwing those stones. I don't like the noise."

"Since when? . . ."

Beatrice regretfully interrupted her game. She pulled her eyebrows together and examined her friend's face.

"I'm sorry, I was only inviting you to play seven stones with me . . . Like we always do . . . Is anything wrong?"

"Why?"

"Why? Why? Why, because you have been playing with your gun for too long," Beatrice replied, staring at her friend's face. His brows bore an expression she could not read. She had never seen this mask before.

She nervously resumed throwing the stones, one after the other in the air and catching them with the same hand, fighting hard to hold her balance, fighting hard not to miss or drop any stone. But, suddenly, the stones deserted her palm as if they had a will all their own. You would think her muscles had been paralysed by the piercing hoot of the night owl. Thin lines of pain graced her smooth, healthy face. You would think she had just heard the drums announce the passing of a loved one.

"What do you mean . . . for too long?" Jikwu asked, venom in his voice, poisoning the very skin on her face. She impatiently wiped off the sweat that seemed to be oozing out of nowhere.

"Well, look at you. That gun is almost completely destroyed. You've been hitting those plantain flaps so hard that there are but a few left. How can you be shooting a gun that has no bullets?"

" . . ."

"Don't stand there and stare at me as if you don't understand what I'm saying. . . . If you want to continue playing guns, then you better harvest another plantain leaf. I'll help you remove the leaves and we can use the stem to make another gun . . . But, on second thought, you have that quiet, murderous look of the lioness on your face at this moment. I can smell it, so you better spare the rest of the plantain farm . . ."

Jikwu did not give Beatrice the chance to finish. He caught her by the neck, squeezing very hard, and they both fell to the ground, Beatrice fighting furiously for her life, viciously clawing at his shoulders. She fought her friend like a tiger, biting and kicking and cursing. She finally succeeded in prying his fingers away from her throat even though he was still pinning her left hand firmly down to the ground with his right hand. She summoned her last breath, punched Jikwu in the nose with her right hand and he screamed in pain, letting go of the other hand. Beatrice threw Jikwu off her body and jumped to her feet. He fell down, his head narrowly missing the exposed root of the pear tree under whose shelter Jikwu had sought sanctuary while playing his game with guns made from plaintain stems. Five plantain stems now lay under the tree, lifeless, all the flaps that served as bullets torn off their green barrels. Beatrice picked up one of the stems, held it in her left hand, and with the back of her right made a sweeping movement along the stem, but the usual twa twa twa twa twa twa that would have been heard if the open flaps were still hanging on the stem was irretrievable. The silence was deafening. She repeated her motion, slowly—once, twice, three times—cautiously watching Jikwu, who was still nursing his nose, wiping away the blood that only he thought was there. Beatrice almost rebuked him but soon noticed he was crying—quiet, gentle sobs that had nothing to do with the pain in his nose. She knew when to hold her tongue. His jaws were shaking, trembling. Jikwu's jaws were set one moment, the next moment he was chewing and grinding on his teeth. The echoes sounded like boulders broken into a thousand little pieces at a quarry. She sat down on the tree trunk, next to the pear tree and waited for the storm to pass. Jikwu finally came and sat beside her, nervously rocking his thighs. His face and arms were covered in sweat. He placed both arms on both thighs, placed his hands on his knees, spread his knees, and began swaying them inward and outward, inward and outward.

"I hear you're going home."

Inward, outward. In. Out . . .

"How long are you going to stay?"

In. Out. In. Out . . . In-out-in-out-in-out . . .

"Well, it will be nice to see your grandparents, enjoy the village . . ."

" . . ."

"Will you be there the entire holiday? . . ."

"It's my mother."

"Is she sick again?" Beatrice asked.

"I wish."

"You wish? What does that mean?"

"Well . . . I guess I can tell you . . . You're the only friend I have."

Jikwu lifted his hands to his face, placing his thumbs under his chin and his index fingers along the ridge of his nose. He was staring straight ahead while he spoke to Beatrice. She was alarmed as she listened to the hoarseness in his voice, for the tips of his thumbs seemed to dig deeper and deeper into his throat, the tips of his index fingers now digging dangerously into his eyes. The tips of his other fingers seemed to be compressing his nose, cutting off the air. He was talking and choking himself right in front of her eyes. She was at a loss what to do. Then, like the heavy August rains, his tears came abundantly. Instinctively, she put her arms around him.

"I knew this was going to happen one day," he said. "Yes, I knew it. When we woke up this morning, my mother was still in bed. That was unusual. She always wakes up before we do . . . My mother wakes up with the cock crows of early dawn . . . not counting how many times she wakes up at night when my father comes home late. It's worse on those nights when he comes home after he's had a lot to drink. He goes from room to room, slapping us on our backs. We hear him shouting, sometimes at no one in particular. When I was younger, we used to jump from our beds and hide under them

when we heard his footsteps trudging toward our room . . .
You know that big scar I have on my back? . . . My father
came home one night and in my rush to find a place under the
bed, I didn't remember that one of the loose springs on the
vono-bed hadn't been repaired. Like Ta Agha's butcher's knife,
the sharp tip slashed through my skin, tearing my flesh. It
hurt a lot. It bled a lot. The next morning, Father didn't even
remember what happened the night before. He didn't even remember my mother treating the wound with iodine.

"Yes, my mother. Sometimes I wonder what it means for a
woman to endure the things I've seen her endure with my father. Do you know that my mother went to school? Do you
know that she's educated? Do you know that my mother used
to work? She used to have an office job. My mother can read,
she can type. Sometimes when she thinks no one is watching,
she pulls out her old typewriter from underneath her bed and
begins typing. Typing on an imaginary sheet of paper. I don't
understand why she doesn't feed the machine with paper. But
she types, types, fast, fast, faster, faster, faster, until the tips of
her fingers hurt. I've seen her blow on the tips of those
fingers, wincing in pain. And after that she quietly returns the
machine under her bed . . . If you ask me, that old typewriter needs some oiling, it needs a good overhaul . . . My
father's eyes have never seen my mother's fights with the machine.

"Where is he? He's never here. He's at the office. He's at
work, he says. He works from sunrise to sunset to feed this
house, to provide for us, he says. Sometimes my mother gets
angry. She tells him, 'Instead of bothering us all the time
about how hard you work, instead of nagging us about how
you work yourself to death for all of us, why don't you let me
go back to work like I used to.' My father decrees that no wife
of his is ever going to work. No wife of his is ever going to

work so long as he's alive on this earth, on this universe of men, women, and children. He claims that a man's job is to work and feed his wife and children, to take care of his family. That's what his father and grandfathers did and that's what he's going to do. The woman's job, he says, is to stay at home, raise her children, cook his food, and entertain his friends. That's what her mother and her grandmothers did and that's what she's going to do. . . . He doesn't lay a hand on her in our presence, but I have heard her quiet sobs and the pounding of fists, echoing like the sounds of our rubber balls kicked against the mud walls. But then, she asks him privately in their room, to let her look for a job. *No wife of mine is going to work for another man,* he says. *No wife of mine will be another man's secretary and that's final. But you have a secretary,* my mother says. *And she is a woman,* she adds. *So what?* my father shouts. *So I'm a different kind of woman. Eeh? Maybe I'm not even a woman. Heh, heh! You must be afraid,* she says. *Afraid of what?* he retorts. *Afraid, yes, scared, because of what you know, because of what you do with your secretary, what you think or are afraid I'll be doing with someone else,* my mother screams right back. *Oooh, so there are two men under this roof, so we've become equals in this house, is that it?* my father says, slapping her. Sometimes, he walks straight through the door. Gone.

"Yes Beatrice, I was expecting this to happen. I'm surprised it took so long. When Mother finally woke up this morning, she didn't seem to remember that we were supposed to go to school. She didn't give me money to buy the puff-puff that we eat with pap, for breakfast, before going to school. When I asked her for money, she couldn't find her handbag. It was lying there, on the table just beside her bed, but she couldn't find it. Even when I picked it up and handed her the bag, she couldn't remember why I was giving it to her. I had to remind her. She asked me to take the money myself and to leave her alone. *Mother, are you sick,* I asked. She stared vacantly at me.

She wasn't seeing me. I didn't seem to exist. I could have been a complete stranger . . . No, even when we don't know a stranger, we still welcome them with a smile. She must have thought I was a ghost. I took the money, went and bought some puff-puff. We had breakfast and went to school. During long-break I ran back home. My mother was sitting in the kitchen, the typewriter in front of her. Today was the first time that machine has left her room. Her fingertips were bleeding and swollen. The paper she'd remembered to use this time was smudged all over with her blood. She was staring straight ahead, talking to herself . . . My mother was talking to herself.

"'. . . Yes, don't you remember? Yes, I did agree to suspend my education, to withdraw prematurely from school, but we also agreed that I would not stay at home. We agreed that I would work . . . Yes, we did. Then I began to work. But then you soon complained. You said all that money that I was making was going to my head. How could money be going to my head? . . . So, money goes to my head because I use it to buy things for myself, for my children, and even for you? . . . With all the money you make . . . I still gave you my money, but you would not be appeased. You had to find a way to stop me from working outside this house. So you dreamed up all these parties, ridiculous functions for which my food and service were put on display for all those men like yourself, those men for whom I cannot work. You claimed that it was part of your job, part of your duty as a big government official to hold these meaningless, long, drawn-out receptions. You claimed it was part of your image, that of a high government official . . . to entertain. You claimed it, you kept up the charade. So I was doing the entertaining, while you puffed your chest out, drank French wine, popped French champagne. How else would you lay claim to this lifestyle and these rights? Jikwu

Andreas, ohhh, what is your name again? J-I-K-W-U—eat-until-you-die—your mother knew why she gave you that name. A mother can feel these things. A mother knows these things. My husband, you have really lived up to your name. All I wanted, all I asked, was be the typist I had become . . . Look at my fingers—they are good at cooking, they are good at sewing, they are good at cleaning, but they can never be good enough for a job outside this house. Well, Andreas, if these fingers cannot be used outside this house, then they can no longer be used in this house—neither can these hands, these arms, these feet, this head, this body . . . nothing.'

"Beatrice, it was terrible. Mother didn't see me. She didn't even sense my presence, this woman who can smell you ten kilometres away. I was standing there, right in front of her, but she didn't utter a word to me. She looked up, she looked around, she talked, she chewed on her fingers, she chewed on her nails. She was hurting herself badly. She was scratching her face, her arms, her neck . . . she was wounding her entire body. I was terrified. I couldn't move. My feet felt very heavy, like two bags of cement. My feet were glued to the ground. I watched my mother in a daze. She was picking up everything in her path and throwing it against the wall. She had a terrible look in her eyes. Not the hollow, lifeless stare I had seen earlier when I listened to my mother's self-talk. I've only seen that particular look once in my life. That was the day she went to the kitchen, took the ax we use for splitting wood, and left the house, not responding to our greetings or any of our worried faces. That day, she calmly and steadily walked twenty minutes to the compound of that woman who was rumoured to be my father's girlfriend and proceeded to demolish the woman's car. Even after my mother was finally brought under control by three men, the ax pried from her hands, the look in her eyes expressed an unspoken but precise determination I can never forget. She didn't talk to anyone for a week. She cleaned us, dressed us, fed us, sent us off to school . . . never saying a word . . . absolute silence. I'd never seen my mother like that. That was then. But today, when I saw her face set in that peculiar fashion as she destroyed everything she could lay her hands on, I was scared of my mother . . . I was scared for my mother. The worse happened when she picked up her old typewriter, threw it on the ground, picked it up, flung it at the wall, picked it up, threw it down, many . . . many times, until she decided to pull the keys out one by one. *Andreas, this is your madness, not mine,* she was screaming, pulling at the keys with her bruised and bleeding fingers.

"I ran to your compound and called for your mother. She came with your aunt and they both did their best to calm my mother down. Beatrice, she tore off your mother's clothes, she tore off your aunt's clothes. She was like a wild animal. Your aunt and mother didn't care that my mother was laying bare their nakedness to the world. They fought to keep my mother quiet, to soothe her aching fingers . . . and then they asked me to find wrappas in my mother's room for them to wear. They sat with my mother, holding her like a baby. They were weeping . . . crying as if my mother were dead. Do you understand this, my my my my mmmm-o-o-o-o-ther was sitting there with them and they were wailing as if she had died. Then the strangest thing happened. My mother looked around and asked them who had died . . . Can you imagine? My mother asked them who had died. Then she noticed for the first time that I was standing there and threw open her arms. I walked dreamily into my mother's outstretched arms. Tears filled her eyes, and then she said to me . . . *You are only named after him, remember that . . . remember to be your own person . . . Be your own person, without killing someone else*

. . . *Did I ever tell you that meker dze story?* she asked me. *You mean the story of that man who was a glutton, the one who would eat and not remember tomorrow? Yes,* she replied. *Do you want to hear it again?* I moved closer and she wrapped her hands around me.

"'There was once a village. A man lived in this village. His name was Chebe. Hmm, Chebe was known throughout the village for his long throat, his greed. Every edible thing that crossed his path, that he laid his hands on, wound its way down his throat. A piece of bone once planted itself in that throat and were it not for Agheyih, the healer, and his timely intervention, Chebe would have been forgotten.

"'Do you remember the proverb that mocks those individuals who have scabies but no nails to scratch them? . . . Well, Chebe was one such fool. He had a kind wife, Male. She knew her husband loved food and she always cooked huge quantities for him. You'd think she cooked everyday for ten children. One day, she cooked some meker dze for her husband before leaving for the farm. When Chebe ate the food his wife had prepared for him, he was still as hungry as that Leopard who was caught in a hunter's trap for three long days until that Monkey came along to save his life . . . But that's another story . . . Chebe took some more of the meker dze, filled a pot, and put it on the fire to cook. When he was certain that the pot of meker dze was well cooked, he drained the water and poured the beans into a small aki. He then added salt, spices, and hot pepper. He put so much palm oil in the beans that you would think it was meant for a new bride or a birth celebration. Then Chebe did the unthinkable. He shut the door! Dead father of mine! He shut the door, in broad daylight. He pulled over a chair, sat near the mortar, and started eating. He ate, and ate, and ate. He watched his stomach bulging out, gaining volume progressively, until he felt pains in his bowels. But he would not stop. Chebe would not keep some of the food for anyone else, not for visitors, not even for his wife. As you can imagine, he did not share with his ancestors either. Chebe must have thought his stomach was as elastic as Mother Earth's. You know what the proverb says, the earth's stomach is never satiated with corpses. We are only human and stomachs do have their own limitations. But what human would shut the world out while they ate? Chebe kept on eating, not noticing the oncoming disaster, then pwaaaaaaaaahhh, his stomach exploded. Much of the food he had been eating slowly meandered its way back into the aki.

"'When Male returned from the farm, she was confronted with the gruesome spectacle. She wept, she cried, she sang, calling for her neighbours, calling on her ancestors:

> My husband is a glutton, oh yang
> My husband is a glutton, oh yang
> If I am the one, I eat and give you some, oh yang
> If you are the one, you eat and give me nothing
> oh yang ke ke le kwo oh yang
> ke ke le kwo oh yang
>
> ndeb ghe eh ndzi nkwu oh yang
> ndeb ghe eh ndzi nkwu oh yang
> a bwo me ma dzi nfia gho o yang
> a bwo gho gho dzi nyub a ghe
> yang ke ke le kwo oh yang
> ke ke le kwo oh yang
>
> My husband eats and dies, oh yang
> My husband eats and dies, oh yang
> When I eat, I share with you, oh yang
> When you eat, you do not share with me, oh yang
> ke ke le kwo oh yang
> ke ke le kwo yang

"'Jikwu, is long-break not yet over?'

"I heard my mother's voice, drifting like a melody, floating over the hills and the trees to me, as if from a faraway, distant land.

"'Jikwu, Jikwu . . . ,' she said my name over and over again, gently rocking my shoulders. 'Wake up . . . It's time to go back to school. When you return, I will be packed and ready . . . Don't look at me like that . . . Last night your grandmother came to me in a dream. That woman demanded to know whose daughter I thought I was. She chastised me for wasting my life, sitting and sleeping in my own vomit . . . It's time to wake up from this slumber and clean myself up. But first, we are going home for a visit.'"

3

Market Scene

Something happened this morning. Something terrible. Terrible, not because it is unusual, but terrible because it happened to my friend. It happened to the one person I have always considered my neighbour, my sister, my friend, ma complice, mon asso, ma kombi. What can I tell you? We came to this strange place many years ago. We were brought here because our husbands had found other kinds of work. We left our farms and came grudgingly. But they enjoyed prosperity and we enjoyed prosperity. Those were the days when the CFA franc carried its own weight. It meant something, it was worth something. This fifty percent devaluation has made the CFA worthless paper, the kind we can take to the toilet and wipe off our waste with. Or as we say nowadays, it's become mere decoration to plaster on our cement walls or close the holes in our brick walls. Nowadays, who talks any more of prosperity.

We are slowly and surely being brought to our knees. Nothing compared to the postures we assume, seated, with our joints clawed by rheumatism or arthritis. We have definitely been brought to our knees. We've been there before, but, tsssssssst . . . this is the ultimate disgrace, the last straw in a line of betrayals. But don't get me wrong. We are fighting, we will continue to fight (a fruitless war, some say, one battle at a time, I say) for as long as we have the strength to breathe fresh air into our lungs. But although we refuse to remain on bended knee, some of us no longer have the strength to fight. Some of us are grudgingly giving up. The bones in their wings have all been broken and the weight is bearing them down, slowly, methodically. Even as they give up, their faces carry that belated smile, hanging on their lips, like that of the cowboy in the Marlboro ad. That is what happened to my asso, ma complice, ma kombi, the only true friend and sister I had in this strange town. We came from two very different regions of this country, but here we found solace, friendship, love, sisterhood. Now look what happened this morning.

As I was sending my children off to school, I peeped through my kitchen window and saw my sister's vegetable basin sitting on her veranda. We usually go, bright and early, to our farms—those small gardens not very far away from our homes just on the other side of the hill—to pick the fresh vegetables that we take to the nearby market every morning, except Sundays, of course. When I saw her basin, full to capacity with freshness, in majestic repose on the veranda, I knew she was ready. She must be giving her children something to eat before going to school, I was thinking to myself, but I did not finish that thought. I couldn't . . .

"Eeeeh kiieeeeh," I heard her voice ring out. "You! These children—if you haven't killed me completely, totally, kaput, you will not leave for school. Uhuum, this is what I left my homeland to come here and . . ." That's my friend and this had become part of our morning calling, our daily breakfast routine. I still don't speak French very well, but I can feel her words. A friend, a sister does. I heard her children giggling. Those little lovable rascals. They know their mother so well,

they understand her. They know how to tune the veins and arteries that like guitar strings play various kinds of music in
her entire body, vibrating through her very soul. They are
used to hearing their mother scold them for trying to kill her
every morning. They're just children. How on this earth of
ours can they kill their loving mother?—they would ask. But
the children also got smart and took their mother's morning
send-off to school in stride. Sometimes they made fun of it.
Sometimes they took the words right out of her mouth.

"Eeeeeeeh, these children . . ."

"Hey, let's go. You know that if we do not leave this house
right now, we'll definitely kill our mother," I heard the eldest
son teasing my friend.

One after the other, the children dashed out of the house.
The oldest child, his school bag half slung over his left shoulder, emerged first from the house, stopped on the veranda and
took a few seconds to gulp down the pap left in his plastic
bowl. He was on the lookout. The moment his mother's head
disappeared into the parlour, he took a swing and expertly
sent the bowl swirling into the kitchen where it landed neatly
on the pile of dirty dishes from the night before. He smiled as
he heard his mother swear, but he made sure he jumped away
from the veranda before calling out to his siblings. From in-
stinct and experience, he knew his mother could suddenly appear from nowhere and pinch his ear, if she was in a good
mood, or pull on it, like a catapult to full tension, before he
could protest or plan an escape.

"Heh, Jeanne, Robert, allons. Pardon allons . . . avant que
la mère nous tue aujourd'hui . . ." Robert dashed out of the
house, running the green comb through his hair, a puff-puff
firmly caught between his teeth, his school bag in one hand.
Jeanne was right behind him, her shoe laces still undone. She
tossed her bag on the floor and bent down to lace her shoes, all
the while grumbling, complaining that her mother should buy

her a new pair of shoes that she would not have to bother lacing every school day morning.

"Mami Joe, goodmorning oh," Paul, the eldest son, greeted me as they filed by my door.

"Eeh gheh, wunna goodmorning ma pikin dem. Wunna don begin di go school?"

"Yes ma." That ended the morning ritual and all the children were gone. When they left, it took us a few minutes to lock up and soon we were also on our way, our vegetable basins resting with carefree abandon on our heads. We were off to the market to sell our fresh harvest, our necks, our backs, our rumps, swaying to the rhythm of our legs.

We chatted as usual. We unburdened ourselves, she in broken Pidgin and somewhat broken French, I in pidgin English and broken French. Sometimes we wished she spoke Munga'ka and I, Fe'fe. We talked about the little things that happened the night before. We sighed, we laughed, we sighed, we laughed. We laughed until our eyes clouded over and the tears came running down our cheeks. You should have seen us. Sibora always knew how to make me laugh, she always knew how to make us all laugh. It was always about her life, always about all the nasty-little-things, as she called them, that had happened to her over the years, pieces of her life, little vignettes that made up a beautiful intricate tapestry. It was the kind of patchwork whose craftsmanship held you captive, in whose presence you were overwhelmed with awe and . . . and inexplicable, profound sadness. Her marriage, her broken marriage, her widowhood, her children, her in-laws, her life here in this strange city. Never have I known a woman transform so much pain into laughter. She taught me a great lesson: Never to let go of those things that nourish our beings, our souls, and make life worth living, despite . . . We could not own or run the world, but we owned our laughter and no one could take that from us, unless . . . unless we let them. It was our aphrodisiac. We had all come a long way from home, we were all in the business of survival but Sibora—she was a special sister, a special kind of woman. Yes, she made us laugh but who is laughing again, who is laughing now? She finally decided she had numbed the pain enough, for too long, for far too long . . . How could you, Sibora!?

We arrived at the market as usual and walked boldly to the turf we had forcefully carved out and made ours over the years. Our friends helped us put our loads down. No sooner had we gone through the motions of greetings, small talk, than we heard the uproar, the first of the morning. We are used to these theatrics that must make their daily unforgettable passage through our lives just as did the masquerades that we all left back home, wherever home was, is. They happen all the time, every time, every day, day in day out. These are our markets. These are the market scenes that like theatrical performances nurture and transform our daily lives. They have become part of our urban existence, just like our daily trips to the market. What can I tell you? But something was different this morning. This particular uproar carried the sounds of a mob thirsty for someone's blood, a mob about to kill. Whose blood were they going to draw so early in the morning?

"Eeh, asso, regardez moi la malchance . . . vraiment, ça c'est la vraie malchance, très tôt le matin comme ça . . . quelqu'un n'a même pas encore posé sa marchandise . . . eeeeh kiié . . . qu'est-ce que c'est que cette malchance comme . . ."

"A say eh, Sibora, leave da your eeeh-kiie palava. Dis people dem go kill some man e pikin today oooooh . . . baluck o . . . for sharp morning time so. A say ee . . . "

But Sibora was gone and I found myself instinctively running after her. The crowd was getting bigger, louder. Screams, shouts, more screaming, more shouting. I strained my ears but I could not hear what Sibora was saying to me. She saw the confusion on my face, grabbed my hand, pulled me closer, and pointed a finger. She's a good seven centimetres taller than I, so I had to raise myself on my toes. What I saw froze the fright in me. Sibora, ever so watchful, was ready for me. The palm of her right hand appeared swiftly, as if from nowhere and she placed it firmly across my mouth. I was suffocating. I couldn't scream. I could feel my teeth chatter, like the teeth of a youngster who's been in the rain for too long on the farm, while the harvest season drags slowly and labouriously to its end. Sibora stared at my face for a brief moment, raised her eyebrows, and then released her palm for a fraction of a second. I took in a deep breath and then she let go of my mouth.

"Eeeehh kié eh kié! wuuuuuuh! eeee kié! wuuuuuulililili," came the women's screams as if from all directions.

"Tu sais, ce sont les vendeurs-voleurs là qui nous cassent les pieds ici tous les jours. J'avais déjà dit, maintes fois, qu'un jour quelqu'un va mourir, mais . . . Allah, on ne me croyait pas . . ."

That was Pauline, our matronly grande soeur. Pauline is a tall, huge, imposing woman. She's big in every imaginable way. She walks with the majesty of the lioness; her body flows, her every move carried with the grace of a giraffe's neck. When she walks, the soles of her feet seem barely to touch the earth; her body floats, flouting the laws of gravity. When she winks at men, there's malice in her eyes, malice captured with provocation on her pouting lips. The men wink back with a hunger in their eyes that remains hanging in the air between them, the only price they know they have to pay if they're to remain in her esteem. The raw, unattainable, unsuppressable energy she exudes, gives them reasons to live, and most of all, warns them not to mistreat her circle of friends. She's been known to punch one or two without regret. When she moves her body, everyone steps aside, or they get carried in the current. Because you see, Pauline walks as if her body were light and spinning, like a quiet tornado, through the rows of market stalls. We cannot measure up to her speed. We have also learned to listen when she speaks. She has represented us many times, more often than we care to count, and the men are afraid, they have learned not to harass us. Pauline rarely lays a finger on anyone. She doesn't have to. She just has a voice and a way with words.

"Na weti di happen, eh?" I asked, nudging Pauline on the elbow.

"Sibora, a telle you say, songting e dong happin oh . . . Da ntip boy dem weh dem di foole woman dem everyday, dem dong killi songone today, wululululululu . . ." We all took up the cry. We were rehearsing the warm-up to the raising of the curtain. We as players were getting ready, preparing to enact and perform that play that would spontaneously come to life and unfold itself without a script. Our basins of vegetables were all but forgotten.

"Yesssoooo, my sisters, let me tell you something," one of our friends put in. "It's not only these vendeur-voleurs of jeans that are killing us . . . Did I tell you about how I was cheated when I went to buy meat? . . ."

"Oh! So that happened to you too?"

"Yes, it has happened to many of us. When you go to the central market, don't be fooled by how attractive the meat looks . . ."

"Uuuuh-huuuh."

"These butchers have devised a method, one you might hardly notice the first, the second, the third . . ."

"Time . . ."

"Yes. I learned my lesson but it came as a terrible blow, at a terrible cost to me. We had our njangi two weeks ago and it was my turn to cook for the group. I foolishly went to Marché Central and bought the required six kilos of meat. I watched the man measure the meat and carefully wrap it up, place the package in my basket, take my money . . ."

"Now, talking about money . . ."

"No, let me finish the meat story first."

"Yes, go on."

"He politely thanked me and asked me—he was all smiles—he asked me to come back next time—and to please remember his stall number . . ."

"Is it stall no. 136?"

"Jesus in heaven, how did you know?" Those of us who had been cheated before knew that Bosco wasn't going to stop anytime soon. Some people have made survival in the city synonymous with the lack of a conscience. Bosco was one of them.

"I got home with the meat and when I took it out of the paper, it looked as if I'd only bought three kilograms. I was so surprised that I took the meat to Anna's, my neighbour who sells flour, and used her scale to measure the meat. Sure enough, I had only three and a half kilos to reckon with. Needless to say, I had to send my daughter to the market for another two and half kilos of meat. Imagine the shame if I had made the njangi food with only three kilos of meat. People would talk . . ."

"Uuuuh-huuh. Of course they would—after all, when you go to their house you are presented with six kilos. You cannot cheat the others, no matter your reasons. Your character would be smeared for life."

"Yes, so I resolved to go to Bosco one more time to see how he dupes people . . . I told him I wanted two and a half kilos of meat-with-bones. He cut out a good slice of meat, to which he added some biscuit bones, took the meat from the scale, and put it on the table near the paper-wrap. That must have been when the switch took place. When he put the package in my basket, I quietly took the meat out."

"Ooooh, a no be tok!"

"He protested of course!"

"Of course. He surely did. He said he felt insulted that I did not trust him. Why was I examining the meat anyway? I tried to tell him that I just wanted to make sure that the amount of meat I had bought would be enough for what I had in mind. I was lying, of course . . ."

"Of course!"

"But behold, when we both looked at the meat, it looked nothing like the meat I'd seen him weigh on the scale. What gave it away especially were the bones. The bones were not the biscuit bones I'd seen moments earlier—I swear to God, just moments earlier. I started screaming abuses at him. He tried to pretend that I was a troublemaker who couldn't pay for the meat I'd ordered and was now harassing a poor honest man like himself for no reason. As you can imagine, our Marché Central people began closing in. The surrounding crowd was getting bigger and bigger and suddenly Bosco threw my money at me with a torrent of abusive words: 'Pars, prends ta malchance et pars d'ici. Je ne veux plus te voir ici. Pauvre femme. Idiote. Villageoise. Tu dois être anglophone. Vraiment, les femmes anglophones-ci sont toujours comme ça . . . toujours à venir nous déranger . . . Pars, anglose . . . go! go witti your baluck, anglose!'"

We all laughed. We were all having a good time.

"You took the money and the meat?"

"Of course!"

"Of course. He was trying to get rid of me before any potential victims caught on to his game. So he could afford to lose that money . . ."

"Than lose his business."

"Of course."

"While we're on the subject of money, you know that there are those ruffians, those thieves in this very market who also trick women out of their money."

"God, it's terrible. They've perfected the art so well that you can hardly tell when you're being conned. Some have learned to disguise newspaper clippings so well that they fool you into thinking it's real money. They usually hide those 'bills' in between real bills in such a way that you wouldn't even think of counting your change, except when you count the money in their presence . . ."

"Even then, when they're good, you can't catch them at their trick. Once, at this very Marché Central, one of those boys gave me back my change. He made me open my palm and he counted the coins, out loud: one, two, three, four, five, six, seven, eight hundred . . . C'est correct, no-o? he asked. I said yes and said good-bye. While waiting for a taxi, I counted the money again. Sure enough I was two hundred francs short. I'm still baffled at how he did it."

"Well, don't be. You saw what happened here today. That woman got fed up with being taken by these smart guys and sought revenge."

Yes, the incident that sparked this early drama will be the talk of the day, maybe two days, and then will fade away like a dream. People will go on with the business of survival, as if it never happened. From what I could glean from Pauline and Sibora, the woman about whom we spoke had come to the market the week before and bought a pair of very good-looking, fashionable, sturdy American jeans for her son. Come Sunday, she had asked her son to wear the new jeans to church. The boy was excited (the four days' wait to feel those American jeans against his body had been painful enough). But in church she saw him in an old faded pair of jeans that looked nothing like the ones she had purchased. She swallowed her pride, controlled her anger, and confronted her son when they returned home from church.

"So, that's why you came late to church. Since you'd decided to disobey me, you chose to wear that tattered old pair of trousers instead of the new ones I asked you to wear . . . By the way, whose hand-me-downs are those you wore to church?"

"What hand-me-downs, mother?"

"Don't toy with me. Whose trousers are those you wore to church?"

"That's the pair of trousers you bought me."

"What? Don't insult my intelligence! You think I'm mad, do you? What's gotten into you? What has . . ." The child did not let his mother finish. He bolted into his room, picked up the plastic bag the pair of jeans had come in and showed it to his mother.

"Mother, this is the plastic I took the jeans out of this morning. This is what was in that package," he screamed, pointing at the pair of trousers.

The poor woman was stunned. With shaky hands, she took the plastic bag from her son. She examined it carefully and then the total realisation of what had happened hit like thunder, hit her like the famous lightning in the grasslands that is known to torch entire herds of cattle. Her head swam in circles. She struggled to focus, to maintain her composure, and think . . . Think, she mumbled to no one in particular. Then she remembered that there were two young men when she walked into the stall. The fluorescent bulb in that particular stall gave a pale blue light that was inviting, tantalising, an ambiance that made everything look chic, expensive, and made the customers feel guilty when they successfully struck a bargain. The woman remembered that the pair of trousers she was shown by one of the attendant boys was not in a plastic bag. She had had all the time to examine it to her satisfaction. After she struck the deal and paid for her merchandise, the boy handed the clothing to his counterpart at the back of the stall and asked him to wrap the jeans for the lady. Seconds later, a semitransparent light blue plastic bag appeared and she walked proudly home, and the pair of trousers she had carefully examined found its way back to its usual spot, waiting invitingly for the next client's watchful eyes. This woman hardly slept a wink last night. She convinced her husband to come with her to the market and exact revenge. That is how we watched in horror as he systematically carved one of the boys up with his knife. The victim's business accomplice vanished when danger reared its head. The police arrived only when it was too late. No one had seen it happen. It had happened so fast, so quickly, like lightning . . .

We were piecing this story together when Sibora suddenly felt the urge to talk about herself, to make us laugh. It was like that with Sibora. Other people's troubles always raised the lid of the basket of problems that she had logged within her heart all these years.

"Well, this woman is lucky. At least she had someone to come fight for her. Look at me, Sibora, sitting here and staring at my vegetables. You all know how I've been struggling and suffering with my children since that man, that devil, that wicked . . . well he's not even a man . . . since he left and shacked up with that pute, that, that . . . bordel . . ."

"Aaaaah! Sibora!"

"Eeeh, is it not true. Eeeh, Mami Joe, ah di lie?"

"No Sibora, you no di lie, but wetin be your own with dis kana story now?"

"Aaaaa, ma kombi, leeeffi me ooooooo!" It was the manner in which she said it. The way she threw her arms up in the air. The way she put her head down, placing her chin inside her left palm and her left elbow on her left thigh. It was the way she looked between her thighs, and with a deliberate effort spat, right there in the middle, a long thread of liquid fired as if from her incisors, aimed straight at the earth, punctuating her story before she went on, that made us laugh. The women laughed. Some of them held their sides for support and Sibora went on as if the laughter was incidental.

"I only discovered two weeks ago that my sixteen-year-old daughter is three months pregnant. I can't feed the ones I already have, now this . . . Agatha, ma voisine, ma kombi, ma sista, you know what I'm talking about . . . I went to the hospital three days ago. I've been having this pain in my chest for quite a while now. I've tried to bear it out. Agatha has scolded me so many times that I should go to the hospital. I finally listened to reason and went to see the doctors. They ran tests and I went back yesterday. This doctor gave me a prescription. He said the drugs will cost about seventeen thousand francs. Eéééééé kié!"

"Wehgheeeh, wich kan trouble be dis now?"

"Yes, that is what I told the doctor. I said, Doctor, as you see me like this, I have no husband. He left me. I found out a few days ago that my sixteen-year-old daughter is pregnant. Doctor, now you are telling me that I, Sibora, will have to buy medicines . . . Doctor, do I look like a woman who has money? The poor man just sat there. He was just looking at me. I said, Doctor, you look at me like this, me Sibora, I do not have any money oooooooo, Doctor, ah swear to God, Allah, Jésus Kri, a no get me money ooooooooooo . . ." And Sibora laughed. We followed suit. She kept on laughing and we kept on laughing, slapping ourselves on the shoulders, on the arms, on our behinds as we added more ingredients to Sibora's story, delving into our own lived experiences. Pauline was the first to notice that Sibora had stopped laughing. She was quiet. Disturbingly quiet. This was so unlike Sibora. As if on cue we all fell silent.

"Eheh, Sibora. What's the matter? Tsssst, aah, stop pulling our legs. You tell us a story, you make us laugh and then you stop laughing yourself. Oooh, stop it. Na weti now, Sibo?"

That was Pauline. Nothing happened. Pauline sighed. Pauline stuck out her fingers and roughly scratched the back of Sibora's left hand. Sibora's left hand fell away. Her head no longer had its support. And then, right there in front of our eyes, Sibora fell on her side. The women started laughing again. Aah, Sibora, your own is too much, some of them said. I will be surprised if one day you don't die laughing, another woman added. Yes, and we might not even know that, yet another replied, bringing to a close the drama and the communion we had shared that day. Some of the women were already moving off, walking slowing towards their conquered spaces. I bent down, took my friend's left hand into mine, tugged gently on it, telling her that it was time to get back to business. Then it dawned on me.

"Wuuuuuuuu! Wulilililili. Sibora, na weti e . . . Eh, Sibora, a beg, no do we so oooh . . . !"

"Na weti, Mami Joe?"

"A beg o, ma sista, come see me sonting ooo. Sibora don die yi ooooo."

"Weti?"

"A say eeeh!"

"Who?"

"Sibora! Ooh ma mami ooo, Sibora don die yi oooo," I screamed.

"Aah, Agatha, you too. Don't start it. It's time to get back to work . . ."

4

The Forest Will Claim You Too

It had taken the young man two weeks to make up his mind. It had taken him two weeks to join the outsiders. It had taken him two weeks to defy the village council. His mother had promptly cursed him, turned her back on him, and wrapped her grief in song. A song sometimes heard blending its melancholy with the groans of trucks roaring through the village.

> *You sit in your house*
> *Trouble marches right in and greets you*
> *You return his greeting but you send him away*
> *You do not welcome him,*
> *give him a wife and a bed to sleep on.*

> *If only the clouds had moved in*
> *If only your father were still alive*
> *I swear, my tears would not scorch my bare chest*
> *I swear, this sorrow would not be eating me alive*
> *I swear, thunder will strike you dead.*

The old woman looked disapprovingly at the two whitemen walking hastily towards her house. One was known to the villagers as the Frenchman, the other, the Asian, who was also invariably referred to as Korean, Chinese, or Japanese, even though some of the villagers claim they had heard him (on one of the rare occasions he had indulged himself with one too many shots of afofo) say he was Korean. It didn't matter to the old woman who they were or where they came from. When she looked at them she saw two strangers, two foreigners, two men whose skins had been burnt so badly by the equatorial sun they looked red-brown, like raw, unripe baby plums. When she looked at them, she saw two vultures who walked around the village as if they owned it. The stamp of ownership was on their crispy foreheads, their bushy eyebrows, their cold, often distant, penetrating stares; it was there in the curl of their lips and the sprint in their legs. When she looked at them, she saw two inflated chests that sat awkwardly on the trunks that gave them support. When she looked at the two whitemen she saw hairy arms, hairy thighs, hairy legs, hair, hair, hair . . . why don't they, oh dead husband-of-mine! cover up all that hair . . . pointing menacingly at her like porcupine quills.

She looked on, disapprovingly, as the two men quickened their pace, walking briskly into her compound. She could now hear their voices. She did not understand the strange words they uttered in their equally strange tongue, but she knew quite well why their footsteps were drawing tracks in the dust, leaving their marks in the red-brown earth in front of her house. She cursed them whenever she heard their feet treading the firm, red laterite that was her own, that was her family's, that was her ancestors'. She cursed herself for being alive to witness what was happening to her village, to her people. For what was happening to her world was worse than anything she could have imagined. There was a time, not so long ago, when she would walk around aimlessly, her eyesight roaming the landscape carelessly, fondling the green slopes around her. There was a time when she could raise her eyes every morning, every evening, and embrace those horizons she could not physically reach but could feel, taste, and touch. There was a time when she would take walks through the forest, hesitantly, like a child discovering the mysteries of the world. She would spread her nostrils, stretch her lungs, and inhale the smells of rotting leaves; stick out her tongue as if to taste the sour stickiness of decaying fruit. She would watch long columns of black soldier ants busily moving food and young ones to new locations—she would sometimes let them bite her big toe but was always careful not to break up their work. She would stand erect, watching the sky for a glimmer of sunlight, her mind playing games, swimming through the tunnels of creepers like water winding its way playfully through the intestines. She had learned the forest's language and would sometimes call on the animals, throwing a greeting here, hearing a response there, as she wove her way through its lush undergrowth. It had always been like that, her relationship with the land, with the forest. It was one at once inviting and sometimes frightening. The forest, tall, dark, dense; where the air was at once pure, inviting her to sing and sleep with the echoes; where the air was also suffocating, forcing her to flee the shadows that crept stealthily around her. The forest, full of secrets that remained inscrutable, impenetrable. But she had learned early enough when she roamed its dense bowels for the leaves and saps that cut off children's diarrhoea, snuffed hacking coughs, sweated malaria through the pores bringing down tropical fevers in record time—these experiences had, like the gentle penetrating heat of a balm on an aching back, eased some of the fear away. The forest had instilled admiration, fascination, respect, awe. Then she went to sleep one night and woke up to a new world, a new forest that had lost the familiar intoxicating smells, one that stood naked like a red, ripe alligator pepper exposed on a torched hill, mourning the death of the shadows that had protected it from scavengers. She could no longer peer without squinting into the valleys and she knew it wasn't her eyesight. A blanket woven of particles of wood, grass, dead insects, and things she could not name now undulated across the landscape, hanging over the village like a ceiling of silky transparent film, hugging the trees, enveloping the skies, colouring the horizons of the entire village. Even the air they breathed sat heavily in their nostrils, weighing down on their lungs. She had slowly learned to despise those who brought this permanent eclipse into their lives.

She was sitting on her favourite mound of bare earth, outside her open kitchen door, directly to the right side of the house, her njagasa tugged between her thighs, her chest bare, her back hunched, when the two men walked up to her. The Korean walked past her, sauntered over to the pepper tree, and started fidgeting with its thick green leaves. The Frenchman observed the old woman for a few seconds, suddenly aware his gaze was bouncing off an impenetrable wall. He pulled a brown handkerchief from his pocket, mopped his forehead, and inquired about her daughter. He's been drinking again, she thought. She could smell the beer on his breath. She continued to play with the nail of her big toe and pretended not to have heard him. At least that was what a stranger who did not know her would have thought. But hidden beneath the lines etched into the aging skin of her cheeks, running from the tails of her eyes, making rainbow curves to the crest of her nose and down to the curve of her lips, was the gentle quiver of silent amusement. Like the villagers, she often "laughed" at the terrible franglais the Frenchman affected when he spoke to them. They knew his pidgin English was tolerable and wondered why he just didn't stick to it. "Dis français na waa oh!" they'd exclaim, shaking their heads. The old woman never laughed out loud but her emotions always remained buried under those mysterious furrows when the man was in her presence. She kept her head bent so low her knees seemed to be holding it in place. She ignored the man and proceeded to peel away the dead skin around the sores that tattooed her legs. (The sores had invaded her body the week after she had buried her son. The customary afuondo treatment had not worked. The weeks had gone by and still no signs of healing. For there was always a new one popping out to take the place of the one that healed. They were spreading like scabies over her thighs, her buttocks, and her back. She was often seen sitting in her yard, her head between her thighs, peeling away at the dead skin, exposing the redness and sometimes the greyish-white pus that oozed from the sores.) She calmly pulled the dead skin off the wound around her left ankle, slowly making a circle from left to right as the skin came off and with one last firm snap ripped it off. She raised the dead skin to the level of her eyes, examined its patched frailness, took in a deep breath, and gently blew it away. At least the dead skin was free, she thought. She turned her head and looked in the direction of the Korean, who was now nervously squeezing one green pepper after another between his right thumb and middle finger. "Tell your friend to stop killing my peppers!" she muttered. Her teeth firmly glued together, she half opened her mouth and tsstsssss, a fine line of spittle shot through the incisors, propelled directly to the bare earth where the white foamy bubbles designed a rainbow arch into the skin of the dark-red laterite. The intensity of her fury suddenly stood erect in the two thick veins that ran down the sides of her thin, long neck.

> Vrom vrom vrom vrom
> Vroooom vroooom vroo roooom vrom vrom
> Vrooooomrooooovrooom
> crack crack crack krakakakraaakakraaaaaaak

wh-h-h-h-h-h-h-iiiiiiiip
Boooooooooooooooooooooooom!
Krakrak krak c-r-a-c-k

Her son had been the first man in the village to join them. He had watched for two weeks as the logging company brought in its machinery, brought in its workers, brought in strangers from other parts of the country. He had heard the rumours, like everyone else, that the pay was good. He had heard the injunction by the village council forbidding any man to join forces with "the forest rapists." How can a man, a son of the soil, participate in desecrating the land that fed his ancestors, the land that now feeds him, the land that will forever feed his family and his kin? It would be like raping his own mother, they maintained.

"Let us ignore them," the village had reasoned. "Let's not feed them, let's not, oh, abomination, show them our hospitality. They will quickly learn they're unwanted guests and will pack their bags, put them in their monster machines, and leave." The elders had poured libation and left the meeting content with themselves.

It was not long before they started hearing the rumours. The old woman's son had been making trips into the forest, where he watched the mighty saws slice through giant tree trunks in the blink of an eye, like bare feet gliding smoothly down a muddy slope; where caterpillars, grunting, rumbling, bulldozed their way almost grudgingly through the forest's thick bed carpeted with thick vines, creepers, and trees, steaming with insect and animal life. He watched in fascination as monstrous mouths opened up, revealing ferocious teeth that clamped firmly around logs like a dog that would not let go of a juicy bone. He watched as the iron teeth picked up the logs, each weighing more than all the houses in the village combined, just as easily as he used to scoop up handfuls of dust to play with when he was a child. He watched as the forest was slowly loaded, piece by piece, onto huge Renault trailer-trucks, the logs so big that only two or three would fit on the flat bed of a trailer. He watched as heavy chains snapped around the logs, encasing them for their trip to the coast. He wondered about their journey across the seas and the oceans, about their imprisonment in the smelly bowels of gargantuan vessels. He often wondered what would happen if the chains broke (they had heard rumours of runaway logs avenging their rape, torture, and confinement). But his worries often vanished when the truck driver jumped into his seat, high up there, and the truck's engine grunted, coughed, and came reluctantly but thunderously to life. He was amused, watching the clouds of black smoke burst through the exhaust pipes as if furious at being restrained for too long, happy at their release from rusty chambers. It made him laugh each time a truck jerked uncertainly to life, throwing the driver a few inches up from his seat until he put the truck in first gear and with one last long groan, the vehicle engaged the tracks on the forest bed, its persistent roar vibrating through the foliage. It was a roar that commanded silence from the insects, the birds, the animals, and the plants as the truck sluggishly meandered its way through the jungle until it exited the village, leaving behind thin rows of black smoke drifting lazily over houses and tree tops. The old woman's son knew what he had to do.

Vrom vrom vrom vrom
Vroooom vroooom vroo roooom vrom vrom
Vrooooomrooooovrooom vroooom vroooom vrooooommmm
crack crack crack krakakakraaakakraaaaaaak
wh-h-h-h-h-h-h-iiiiiiip
Booooooooooooooooooooooooom!
Krakrak krak c-r-a-c-k

Dead Father of Mine!
Darkness has fallen
But they won't stop
Why can't they stop?
Why can't we stop this?
the sacredness of the night
the pregnant silence of dusk
is consumed
we sit
and watch.

They were gathered in the small off-licence bar, the one spot in the village where simple goods for daily use—tinned tomatoes, Maggi cubes, salt, matches, soap, razor blades, kerosene—could be bought. It was also the place where they met in the evenings to drink, sometimes listen to the radio— more often the BBC and sometimes, the VOA—or dance to very loud music, this, when more than half of the room was already inebriated. Ajasco's Off-Licence, better known as "Eyes Coal Bear" was the social spot, the community centre. Ajasco had once visited his brother in the city, the story goes. They had gone to bars every day and he had listened to men order one cold beer after another. Ice cold, they would emphasise. He had scoffed at cold beer. Who drinks cold beer, he asked. Beer tasted like beer just the way it was. If this was civilisation, then it wasn't meant for him. He had come back from his visit and the villagers had watched as he carefully scripted a new name below the old one: Eyes Coal Bear, it read. The villagers didn't know what to think. Ajasco thought it was quite funny. Eyes Coal Bear had become the one place they all went to be informed of all that had happened during the day while they were away taking care of the business of living. Wives often barged in to drag their husbands home but usually not before they themselves had sat down for a bottle of beer or two. Children often ran into Eyes Coal looking for their mothers, ready to complain about one thing or another. Ajasco kept the atmosphere festive, his voice the loudest of all as he navigated between his customers, bottles of beer, glasses of palmwine, or afofo cups in his hands, sharing a kind word here, a booming laugh there. The villagers loved him. His bark was louder than his bite, they claimed, although they were also in awe of his anger when debtors could not pay their long-standing debts. He had put long benches along the walls and the villagers would come in, extend greetings to those already seated, and then secure a place for themselves. This evening was no different. They were talking, some singing, the radio blaring on as they sipped their drinks from glasses or as most did, drinking straight from the beer bottles. Ajasco's big tilly-lamp hung bright from the ceiling, wearing a complex tapestry woven around its base by the insects that flew about energetically, embracing its warmth and brightness.

It was almost five minutes past seven and Ajasco proceeded to increase the volume. Every Wednesday evening, they all listened religiously to *Reflections*, a five-minute editorial presented by a journalist they all called the Son of the Soil. The Rambler, for that was what he called himself, reflected on the issues, mostly social and political, that took up five minutes of his air time once a week. His ramblings had been yanked off the air more times than anyone cared to count, but even after serving short jail terms, he walked through the prison gates and went right back to rambling. He seemed to have more fire in his belly and drums rumbling in his ears after each incarceration.

Good evening ladies and gentlemen, greetings to all of you out there. Today is a very sad day for the Rambler, for us all. A sad day indeed! God knows I have seen many such days, but today's sadness weighs me down as if ten bags of cement have been tied to my legs. I

almost didn't make it to the studio and this is why: there was a terri-
ble accident in Mutengene last night. An accident in which a timber
. . . yes, one of those infamous timber trucks got out of control . . .
The driver lost control of the truck as he came down that little slope
of hill at the Mutengene-Limbe junction and ploughed into people.
The official word is thirty dead, but my sources tell me the toll is
much, much higher. We all know the throngs of people that are al-
ways on the move in that busy area. One family alone lost a mother
and three children to the timber truck. As you would imagine, the
truck driver and his motor-boy vanished into thin air before the
crowd realised what was happening. So this evening we mourn. The
Rambler mourns with you. We mourn because Mutengene, that
lively little corner that is always teeming with life, will never be the
same again. We mourn and ask ourselves when this is all going to
stop. It's not enough that our forests are vanishing every day. It's no
secret that there has been more logging in the past three years than
there has been in the thirty years that preceded them. And what are
we being told? No harm done! The forest is overpopulated! Yes, my
people, our forests have a disease we all share: they are suffering from
overcrowding just as the so-called third world is crumbling under
the weight of overpopulation. The rape of the forests therefore is not
environmental genocide. This rape is supposed to bring relief and
regeneration, we are told. Fell down the trees and we no longer suf-
focate and everyone can breath freely, happily! Why is there no policy
for a sustainable harvest? We need not ask why. We need not wonder
why trees are not planted to take the place of their fallen parents. We
have our answer: overcrowding. It doesn't even matter that our land
has some of the rarest species in this so-called global village of ours.
So our land is paying for crimes it did not commit. We are also pay-
ing with our lives, with the blood of our mothers, wives, sons, daugh-
ters. We have become the proverbial father who gives his daughter
away and still has to provide the bed on which his son-in-law will
sleep with her to give him grandchildren. A few months ago, this
business with the timber trucks on our highways was getting so bad,

the outcry so loud that the powers-that-be thought it wise to move the loot by rail. That gave the illusion of a decline in the exportation of timber to those of you who could no longer count a truck for every step you took on the highway. That at least cut down on the accidents that occurred as driver after driver rammed their cars into these death traps. To top it all, the exploited populations have no roads, no schools, no hospitals, no pipe-borne water . . . you name it. Some of them are being evicted from the very lands their families and generations of their ancestors have inhabited. And so, when we see our forests dwindle away each day, we wonder; when we see our people grovel even more in poverty as the trees float through their neighbourhoods, float even further on our waters, we wonder even more; when we see our people left out in the rain, we hold our breath; and when we hear the cries of our children, our fathers, our mothers, when we hear their lungs, hearts, brains, pop through their flesh as the trees from their own homelands flatten them to a pulp, we know it is time to invoke the proverbial downpour that must run through the land in the heart of the dry season in order to drench it and appease the thirst of the gods who wreak havoc using the hands of the sun. That our leaders can permit such atrocities is no longer what I worry about. We know where they stand. They have to do what it takes to stay in power. We ought to ask ourselves (and this is what I worry about), how can we let the French, the Thais, the Italians, the Germans, the Koreans . . . how can we let these outsiders, who protect their own, walk in here and crush us with our own. What I ask of you is this, What are we going to do about it? What are we willing to do about it? Just the other day, at that franco-phoney summit, one of my colleagues asked the French president where he had buried his conscience, why so-called foreign investors were so disrespectful of our . . .

Ajasco slowly turned the knob. Click! Time stood still. The hair on their bodies remained standing at attention. Invisible paws crawled through the room, tearing at their flesh.

Vrooooooooooom! Vrooooooooooom! The graveyard silence in the room broken by the vromvrom vrooooom of saw engines that only moments ago had been an irritable nuisance, now sounded like a war cry in a distant collective dream.

"Wulilililililili!" came one woman's subdued cry.

"Wulilililililili!" another responded lamely.

"Na so, my sista dem. Na sooo," a man replied, his head bent so low the palmwine in his glass spilled on the floor, soaking through the toes of his right foot. He rocked his head from side to side, as if responding hesitantly to a makossa tune.

"Na so oh. Na dis palava wey we soso talk say trouble go must cam commot some day. We no know sey trouble dey only for we corner . . ."

"Na so oh, my broda. Trouble dey only for we dumut, we no di see am . . . No bi na dis baluck wey dis wunna frenchman . . ."

"Uh-huuh, le soi-disant frère du président français ou même il se dit qu'il est même quoi oh, avec son soi-disant frère de Hongkong . . . n'est-ce pas c'est comme ça qu'ils sont en train de nous tuer ici au village . . . ?"

"Na so, my broda. Today we hear sey na Mutengene, tomorrow no be na we, uum?"

"True, true. Small time e go be na we oo. For day time sef, man no fit see sun for sekop say whiteman dem de cut all we firewood carry am go fix whiteman contri, we dey here we di die. Umm? No be na we pikin dem don die for Mutengene so . . . ?"

"Na weti we go do now?"

"Weti you mean na weti we go do now? . . . Ting weh we get for do now na for drive dat whiteman dem make dem commot for here. Wunna go only shiddon here say, 'na weti we go do now?' Na wich kana baluck dis now?"

"Ah swear, Massa Peter, ah tink sey you di cresh . . ."

"Ah say eh papa Allen, ah di crish na how? . . . for sekop

sey ah don talk say make we drob whiteman, you say ah day cresh?"

"Yes, crish day for your head. If we touch whiteman now, no be gobna go send soldiers dem make dem come catch we go put we for guaroom. Ah beg oh, me a no fit go me prison again . . ."

"Yes, no be so? *Ah no fit go me prison again.* Wunna see me de baggah! Make we only shiddon here de fear prison, de drink mimbo . . ."

"Yes, and gather your tails between your legs like frightened dogs . . . and you call yourselves men! . . . men with no testicles between their thighs . . . Listen to all of you. Na-weti-we-go-do, na-weti-we-go-do? But wunna sabi shiddon drink palmtree . . ."

"Di drink afofo sotey we piss for we closs . . ."

"Di drink mbuh! . . ."

"Di drink '33' . . ."

"Uh-huum, all we talk dey na only inside Satzenbrau, inside Guinness, inside Beaufort, but make correck talk sleep for ground, all man di run hide inside bush like say kwefo di cam. Wunna no di shame sef!"

"Mantrouble, na weti? You want say make we do weti?"

"Ah beg leave man, make man drink e jobajo."

The laughter from the group was lame. They looked nervously at Mantrouble, who was standing, arms akimbo, holding Teresa's son firmly against his waist. His eyes were red as if he had been smoking banga and that redness burnt a hole through the skull of every man sitting in the room. Suddenly, the little boy began to cry.

"Theresa," Ajasco called. "Teresa . . . wusai da Trisia deh? Wunna call am make e take dis timber baby from here," Ajasco repeated nervously.

"I swear to God! One of these days I'm going to walk into that forest, take one of those giant saws into these small hands of mine, and open up that white kanda . . . I'll rip his chest open, man-to-man. I'll lay his bowels bare for the ants to feed on. Yes, I'll do it. That's the language he understands, the only language they will understand . . . And he thinks we're fools and that's because we've let him . . . I'll do it and then we'll see what your government can do . . ."

"Ooho! It's now our government?"

"Uh-huh, isn't it your government . . . eh? Isn't it?"

"My brother, we're all Cameroonians. It doesn't matter what part of this country we come from . . ."

"It matters to me. That man sitting next to you is one of them. They own this country . . ."

"My brother, let's not say things we'll regret in the morning. Massa Allen is our brother. He's lived here with us for more than I can remember . . ."

"Uh-huh."

"So let's not misuse our anger . . ."

"You're right. This is exactly what Mi Nshieh—mother of the earth—predicted when those people came here. She had not even closed her mouth and look what happened . . .

>*The forest has*
>*claimed him claimed him claimed him*
>*the forest has claimed my son.*
>
>*The forest has*
>*claimed him claimed him claimed him*
>*the forest has claimed our child.*
>
>*The forest has*
>*claimed him claimed him claimed him*
>*the forest is eating its children.*

The moment they heard from the Rambler, their voices suddenly rose in song as if their souls had been waiting for release. Some remained sitting, singing with bowed heads while others sluggishly raised their weary bodies, singing, dancing, shuffling their feet as they mourned the dead. This song was the gift Mi Nshieh, the old woman, had given them. The first verse had been the only words to escape her mouth that gruesome day in the forest. They had claimed her song and made it their own.

Yes, the old woman's son had been the first man in the village to join the group of loggers who had come from afar. Mi Nsieh had warned her son: she had *seen* his death, she had said. It was wrong of him to join hands with these vultures, she had warned. But her son had not listened. The attraction of the giant saw; the buzz buzz buzz, the jawbreaking buzz-z-z-z-z that dared the forest, the earsplitting vroooooom vroorooooom that dominated the forest; the giant teeth that cut through centuries-old trunks of natural steel in a matter of seconds like child's play; the fascination of watching these ancient equatorial giants come toppling down booooooom; the raw power he felt as he moved the giant saw around the trunk anticipating the moment the wound he made in the trunk snapped crack, crack, cracracracrack just like a dry twig, had been too powerful to resist. He had been hired and taught how to use the saw and he had excelled. But that day had come. His mother had been alerted of the tragedy. She had refused to sit at home and wait for her son's body to come to her. His body was still lying where it had been found by his coworkers. They had gone to the village for more hands instead of using a tractor or chains to move the huge branch and free his body. Mi Nshieh had looked at her son's body, what was left of it. He seemed to have no chest. All of his body right up to his head had been completely swallowed up by the earth, the skin of his face lay flat on the ground like the lid of a pot; his intestines, lying to the side of his body, were thankfully covered by a crust of black ants. His right knee had been crushed and the bone stuck out menacingly. The old woman had bent down, pushed the bone back under the flesh, stood up, turned around and her song

>*The forest has*
>*claimed him claimed him claimed him*
>*the forest has claimed my son.*

had propelled her steps back to the village. She had buried her son, the village had buried its child, but the bad-talk had stayed. Some claimed the death of the boy was direct punishment—for how come, they queried, had the only Cameroonian to die been a true son of the soil? How come, they reasoned, had his mother, the woman whose hands heal everything they touch, how come the sores had taken to her body like a plague? Some claimed he had been murdered with witchcraft by his workmates, for it was no secret they had to protect themselves with the help of reputable medicine men to be able to work for the whiteman. Still others claimed the old woman, the one person in the village who *knew* the herbs and the plants more than anyone else, must have killed her own son. She had warned him right from the beginning. She had *seen* it. She had refused to talk to the whitemen who had come to ask her permission to hire her son. She had spat on them and asked them never to set foot in her compound again. But the men had returned. They needed to have the old woman on their side. The Frenchman had initiated a relationship with her daughter, believing this would make the old woman happy, grateful, malleable. It had only made things worse. For Theresa had had one of those eight "timber babies," born since the arrival of the logging company, that the villagers so hated. Two had thankfully looked liked everyone in the village but the others, well, were the others. They were babies who in their innocence had bit by bit been fueling the flames of rage that burned silently, furiously, like a savanna night fire in the hearts of the villagers. They emptied their hatred into the babies, whose mothers, their daughters, were being conquered along with the land. Four timber babies had died long before their second birthdays and there were many rumours too about the true causes of death. Malicious tongues rumoured they had seen Mi Nsieh place those babies out in the night on those round stumps of wood her son had made for her to use as chairs— those stumps she had abandoned in the open to endure the fury of the rain and the sun. But these were rumours. Death here was never by natural causes.

One man, Mantrouble, had stood behind his timber baby. He had continued to nurture his love for Theresa and had sworn to avenge the fate of the child. Today he knew that day had come. The villagers could sense it. They had always known Mantrouble would be the match that would light the gunpowder. Now was the time to lift their guns and fire. So, that night, under the cover of darkness, they each ran errands. A group of young men were assigned to demolish the roads to prevent any timber trucks from coming into or leaving the village. An easy job for young men who early in life had learned to tamper with roads in the rainy season to supplement their incomes—they always made deep potholes on the roads so that the pickup trucks, few of which had four-wheel drive, would get stuck and the drivers who drove into the villages to buy foodstuffs to take back to the cities would have to pay them to push their trucks out of man-made traps. The drivers knew the game. They always came prepared. It had been easy to blackmail the mechanic into disabling the caterpillars that hauled the timber onto the trucks. The two men who walked into his house that night had quietly recounted the story of the annual end-of-harvest ceremony that was held in the village. Rumours held that human testicles plucked from an outsider were used as the main ingredient in the rituals. When his coworkers heard the news, they left everything they owned and vanished into the stillness of the night as dark shadows went from house to house delivering the message. This was one message that could not be conveyed with the drums. Drum language would carry their plans far beyond the forest and warn their enemies. The last duty fell on Theresa. This was the one thing she could do to redeem herself in their eyes. Their plans hinged on the job the old woman had to perform with the hair. Teresa had always kept the locks of hair she found on the floor when she cleaned the house of the whitemen. She enjoyed the game she played with the hair she collected—she would place strands on her forehead, use a broken piece of comb to hold the clump of hair into her own roots and then comb the hair down over her eye. It always tickled and made her giggle. She did not have to be persuaded to give the hair up. The women gathered at Mi Nshieh's compound and talked in whispers as she poured libation, reciting one incantation after the other, invoking their gods and their ancestors to come to their aid.

The morning stood perfectly still when the two whitemen scurried into the old woman's compound. They were nervous, they were sweating, their faces were red like the fireball of sunset. The silence was overwhelming, it was suffocating. This was a silence they were hearing for the first time. It was a silence broken jarringly by the intermittent chirping of insects, of birds, of the wind rustling through leaves and trees. The old woman interrupted her game. She stopped peeling off the dead skin and began to play with her big toe, running her index finger over the nail she had painted pitch black.

"Mami, we come see you because work people tous partis. Dem don vanish . . . whiiiiip . . . like that (he clicked his fingers). Mami, wusai all people don partis? . . . Mami, you must helep we . . . Mami, talk for me now. Parle. Parlez, to me. We must finish dis work ici, quick quick . . . Where all man done go now, Mami?"

She played with her big toe. The other man played nervously with the green peppers. He wondered what concoctions had darkened the stumps of wood but he knew from looking at them it must be a bad omen. He turned around and pulled on the European's arm.

"No, we can't leave. This woman is our only hope."

"No she isn't," the Asian replied. "The longer we stay here, the more time we waste. We better get a message to town before it's too late. God knows what this witch has done . . . Who would have thought they would betray us like this?"

"What do you expect? They're all thieves, liars . . ."

"Where's Teresa anyway?"

"I don't know . . . she's probably gone where the rest have. How would I know? The mother won't say a word . . . Look at her! The, the, the . . ."

"I can't stand it . . . Where are you? Where are all you monkeys?" he screamed. "Come out of your holes! Show your faces, you, you . . ."

"Sortez de vos trous, imbeciles!" he screamed. "Eh oui, c'est comme ça. Vous voulez toujours tout pour rien, merde! . . . bande d'imbeciles, bande de feignants, faites vous voir."

"We have to get out of here before it's too late."

"It's never too late," she replied. "The forest has claimed our children and now the forest will claim you too," she said quietly, her eyes flat, emotionless, like the eyes of a king cobra poised to strike.

The two men had been in the equatorial forest long enough to know what they were witnessing.

Theresa walked out of her mother's house, carrying Alienze—the-one-who-looks-and-sees—on her back. "I will take you to the men," she said.

When the soldiers arrived, armed to the teeth, they found one lone person, sitting on a stump of blackened wood. The body of a rigid old woman, marked with scars; covered in sores, some fresh, some festering, some healing; a body adorned from her waist to her thighs in colourful rows of jigida, her breasts flat on her chest—this, the only semblance of life that welcomes them. They knew a suicide when they saw one. Why would she commit such an abomination? they asked. They fled, accompanied by the eeriness of what lay cloaked in the tranquility of the forest and the grating laughter from the hollow cage of her emaciated body.

5

Election Fever

Election time
election time,
na time for election
let-us-play.

The elections are coming. There is excitement in the air. Let me try to describe what it feels like. You know what happens to children in the dry season when the first rains come? We always wait with a lot of expectation. We wait, our muscles tense, our armpits sweaty. We wait . . . and the wind finally rages in, blowing away uncontrollably, plucking dry leaves from branches, sweeping up dust in its path, and furiously mixing them up. The howling wind carries the debris around, swirling through the tree tops shaking their branches in welcome. We run outside, we run around the nsaa, sniffing the air, playing *guess guess how strong the rain will be*, betting on *there will be hailstones, there will be not*, laughing at the groans and the sighs seeping through the branches and leaves, imitating their whiiing whiiiing whiiiiing sounds. My mother! We get so excited we can taste the rain before it comes pelting down. We wait feverishly, sweat rolling down the hollow of our spines as what looks like a million stalks of elephant grass advance steadily, marching determinedly like crazy soldiers across the valleys, the hills, and over the trees, running a race we can never ourselves compete in. The sight of those spiky, silvery creatures approaching makes us wild with pleasure. Unable to control ourselves, incapable of controlling our nerves any longer, we tear off our clothes and invade the nsaa, rolling ourselves in the dust, daring the rain with invectives at every provocation by the first few wet drops, our little dark bodies turning into various shades of brown, our kinky hair tattooed in spots as if an invisible hand had deliberately made those patches with baby-pancake (that's our name for brown powder, like the one my mother uses on her face on Sunday before going to mass). When the first real downpour finally sprinkles the dry earth all around us, our throats are so dry, our screams seem to be coming from other children in other compounds. The hoarse sounds from our sore throats blend unceremoniously with the drum language of heavy rain drops on the zinc rooftops. We squeal, we scream, we sing, we dance, we stick out our tongues, wagging them wildly, competing with each other at catching the most drops with the tiny red tips of our tongues. Tegheh kwu! You should see us when the first hailstones, like the heads of two dozen blunt needles, land on our exposed black-brown skins. Our hysteria, bottled up until then, breaks loose. We fight each other, vying for the same frozen stones, even though they are everywhere. You know what? I think the sky must have a good refrigerator. (My mother says I should stop this silliness but she also confirms that the sky uses its freezer sparingly.) When we are lucky and she is kind enough to give us a lot of ice, we simply lie on the bed of cool rocks, we shut our eyes firmly to protect them from the wrath of the other stones still pelting down on our bodies, tearing through our skins; we make sure we shut them tight, spread our legs and arms, and wait. We wait, silently. Then, gradually, we giggle as the rocks melt, the cold water tickling our bare backs, bare buttocks, and wet calves. We play a game with our toes, opening our eyes for brief moments to judge who can move theirs the fastest. Spread-eagled on our backs, we are often lost in our own worlds. We are always oblivious to the adults, who watch with consternation as plantain leaves are shredded into a thousand thin, long pieces by the hailstones. We often do not notice when the rain stops, when the heavenly cotton balls beneath our bare backs turn into pools of cold water. We often do not hear our mothers screaming, "wake up," "go clean up!" We are always downcast as we wash off our bodies the designs left by our visitors from the skies. But that does not stop us from carefully saving our anticipation to await their brothers and sisters, who must come looking for them in the near future.

Our experience with hailstones is the only thing comparable to the excitement that I see in the adults around me as election day approaches. I am thirteen years old, so I cannot vote, but I do see what these elections are doing to big people. They are excited, they are as anxious as we are when we see and hear the wind above our heads, swirling around our compounds, generously spraying everything in its path with debris; but their anxiety does not always seem to signal the kind of gratification that we expect when the first hailstones hit our bare bodies.

My uncle and my grandmother are the two persons that I watch most closely during election time. Oh! my uncle, Uncle Alienze. All the children call him Uncle or Uncle Alienze but the adults just call him Aliii, dragging out the iiiii sound depending on their mood that day or how they generally feel about him—if and when they do see him. Uncle Alienze is a very funny man. He always tells us stories about strange places and strange people. He plays with us, he knows how to make children laugh, but most people in the family do not like him. It isn't really that they dislike him as much as they don't like his ways. That's because Uncle is a strange man. He is married, he has a wife and three children. But Uncle often leaves the house and vanishes into thin air. That's what Auntie Maggie, his wife, always says. When Uncle Alienze takes off like that he never tells anyone where he is going, not even Auntie Maggie. He disappears for weeks, sometimes for months, at a time and when he reappears, no one knows where he went, what he did, why he has come back. Not even his wife, Auntie Maggie. I have noticed that no one asks him anymore where he had been, not even Auntie Maggie. People just go around doing their things as if Uncle had not gone anywhere. I once asked my uncle what his job was and he said, "I do business." And that's what people in our family say, "He does business." But my grandmother says he is a fool. My grandmother once said to me, "When you see that fool crawling back into this house with his tail between his legs, if he has one! (my grandmother interrupted herself and spat, straight between her legs), that means he's squandered what little money he made. The damn fool! How did such a thing come out of my loins?!" she exclaimed, and shot another line of spit between her legs, followed by a long drawn out sigh. Only Mi-andee can sigh like that. She can beat any one in a sighing competition any time. Oh, Mi-andee! That's my grandmother. Everyone calls her Mi, meaning mother, grandmother, but we the children call her Mi-andee, meaning eldermother, grandmother; mi-wa-ndee—mother-who-is-older. Mi-andee can be very outspoken. She is fond of saying wicked things about her children, not just about Uncle Alienze. How can she say such cruel things? But she is the only one who can talk about my aunts and uncles like that. Who else can dare? The funny thing is, Uncle Alienze does not seem to care much about what

Mi-andee says, especially at a time like this when big people are campaigning and politicking all over the place. You should see Uncle during election time. He is what we call a bizi-bodi. He goes from home to home arguing with people about politics, which party will win, which one will lose, which ones will lose "badafully." Badafully! You should see him chuckle, looking pleased with himself when he says b-a-d-a-fully. Ah, Uncle Alienze! You should see him, talking, shouting, gesticulating, spitting on people—all about politics. This thing called politics makes big people crazy and election time just makes them crazier.

An uproar broke out this morning in our compound. If someone had told me that another uproar would bring our day to a close, I would have said that you cannot cut a worm into two and both ends grow back to full length in the same day. But that's exactly what happened. The commotion began when Uncle Alienze emerged from his house and stepped into the nsaa. He was well-dressed. He was wearing that purple pair of trousers that I know he likes very much. Auntie Maggie hates them. "Who wears purple trousers," she would ask? "What man, what real man, wears purple trousers?" she would say, her loud voice addressing the entire compound, her left hand on her waist, her right hand up against the door. But you know Uncle. He would take his time, iron his trousers until all the wrinkles have been flattened out and all you can see are two sharp lines running down the front of the trousers and two sharp lines pointing down the back of the trousers. Uncle had also taken extra care with his hair this morning. It was well-oiled, well-combed, and pressed down in the appropriate areas to give it the shape he loved. (This is the hairstyle he wears when he says he feels "groovy." I wish my uncle could feel groovy more often.) Frankly, I find it very funny when he combs his hair like this. Mi-andee says he takes more time combing that hair than finding his way back home. You should hear the sneer in her voice! My uncle is a very hand-some man but his head looks too big, if you ask me. My grand-mother says it is because of the "afro," that mound of hair my uncle carries on his head. No man in our family wears their hair that big. She claims there was a time when young men and women used to wear afros and they outgrew that crazi-ness, but her son remained trapped in it like the mosquito doomed to spend its life bugging the ear. But my uncle's hair and purple trousers were not the only things that attracted the entire compound's attention.

My uncle was wearing the uniform of the "Cry Baby Party," also known as CBP. No one refers to that party by its real name. CBP's president goes on the radio constantly to com-plain about the badaful things that are said about his party; that's how his party got the nickname. Tegheh kwu! That man likes the word *slander*. Whenever he's on the radio he says people slander his party too much; they slander his wife, they slander this, they slander that . . . so the children nick-named him Mr. Slander. We think it's very funny, calling the president of a whole party Mr. Slander. My father claims that CBP has two members: the president of the party and his wife. (Sometimes I think my father is worse than his mother.) He also claims that CBP is a "mushroom" party that has been cre-ated and funded, just like many other small opposition parties, by the ruling party. The emblem of CBP is the tiger, a fero-cious, growling tiger, its paws like sharp claws ready to strike. You should see the glee in their eyes when the big people talk about CBP. You can therefore imagine our surprise when my uncle came out that morning, the CBP tiger growling from his chest. I don't know what must have possessed him. You see, unlike everyone else in the family, my uncle belongs to PU, at least that's what we had always thought. One day he shocked everyone when he appeared wearing the colours of the People's Union.

"PU is the way to go," Uncle proclaimed, parading around the nsaa, showing off his new party uniform. "It's the party that has a history of struggle written in blood. Its leaders were the first political martyrs of this country, long before independence. PU is definitely the way to go." He went on to add that people in my family should be ashamed of themselves for not acknowledging the sacrifices of PU.

"My son, we're well aware of their sacrifices. Do you think we're stupid?" my grandmother retorted. "But they can't do anything for us now. They think all they need to do is dredge up that old history and we'll come flocking after them. Well, my son, that's not enough. And by the way, they're so tribalistic!"

"Tribalistic? Who isn't in this country?" my uncle asked. "Tribalism is the rule of the law in this place. Every party segregates, either on the basis of where we come from or the languages we speak. That's why you're all chanting this Power-to-the-People nonsense. We're all tribalistic! And by the way, PU is the real opposition, not this nonsense you PP people think you are. You fool yourselves that you are the most popular, the most democratic party, your leader the best thing that has happened to this country in a long time, but just wait and see. We're biding our time. Power to the people, my __!" I can't repeat the word he used.

Yes, every single member of our family belongs to the party nicknamed Peuple, and that's why they could not forgive Uncle Alienze his defection.

"In this family, we are PP people," my grandmother would say. "Our life of suffering is over—sofa don finish—that's who we are. We're saying thirty years of dictatorship is enough. What are you PU people saying? This country has the blood of your leaders on its hands, so what? Are you PU murderers not going to do the same thing tomorrow . . . Eeeh? You tell me . . . We're saying thirty five years of suffering is enough. We're going to take back our country. What are you PU people saying? Maquis maquis maquis, blood blood blood. That's all you PU people are. Wunna see me some maquisards dem! . . . We're saying forty years of . . . ," and as she spoke, the number of years kept on increasing, steadily. But you know my uncle. This kind of talk glides over his head like water on a duck's back. The uproar in our compound swept over him like rain clouds rolling over the city. He walked away, whistling to himself like wind sailing through treetops. Auntie Maggie, straight as an Indian bamboo, was standing on the veranda. She watched as people talked. She watched as her husband walked away without a word escaping her pouted lips. She smiled, shook her head, and said, "Dis kana one wey Alienze don commot for house for sharp morning time so, e mean say njoh money dey for someplace." And she laughed heartily.

"Ah no be talk!" her mother-in-law exclaimed, and the two women burst out laughing.

"Big Mami, no worry yourself. Ah go only wait yi for here make e come back with that money."

"My pikin, you go see the money?" my grandmother asked, laughing and shaking her head.

"Ah no go see am say weti. Big Mami, no play with me, oh. This one na politick money. And ah must chop politick money, if no be so ah go kill some man e pikin."

"Ah beg o, no kill my pikin, ooooo," my grandmother said loudly, but the two women just laughed and laughed, holding their waists, their legs akimbo, tears in their eyes. I didn't think it was funny. Laughing about killing my uncle. I know he is a strange man, some say he is a bad man, but I also know he is a good man. Deep down he is a good man. He is just strange in his own way. Strange enough to confront us with a hungry, angry CBP tiger so early in the morning. Hmmm, wunna see me some baluck oooo!

Things calmed down after my uncle walked away. But later that morning, after I had finished eating with my grandmother, she asked me to accompany her to one of her meetings. My grandmother spends much of her time at all sorts of meetings: njangi meetings where women go to eat, gossip, and save money, and quarter meetings of all sorts—subsection party meetings, development meetings, adult school meetings, PTA meetings (I have no idea why she attends PTA meetings—after all, all her children are grown. She claims she has the right because all her children attended the neighbourhood RCM school). Then there are birth, wedding, and all the death celebrations she religiously attends and makes money and food contributions. (My grandmother claims the entire country will come out and bury her when she dies and she will be watching them from heaven above and woe betide those who do not show up! God forbid! I think she will strike them with thunder.) If you ask me, Mi-andee attends too many meetings. She sometimes takes me along to carry her bamboo stool. She hates to arrive at a crowded compound and not have a chair to sit on. She therefore takes me when she suspects that might be the case.

All my grandmother said was she had an important meeting to attend. She would not give me any details. (As if I wouldn't know just by looking at her. Mi-andee likes to joke with me like that.) I carried the stool in my right hand and walked with her. But something strange happened just before we got to the meetinghouse. About two houses away from the building, my grandmother disappeared behind a house. I thought she was going to urinate, but to my greatest surprise she reemerged from the back of that house looking very different. She was wearing one of the strong opposition party uniforms! . . . Where had she been hiding it? It must have been tucked deep down in her handbag.

"Shut your mouth before you swallow a fly!" she commanded.

Her words seemed to be floating to me from the roof of the house. My grandmother? Mi-wa-ndeeeeee?

"I said, close your mouth!"

She roughly pulled my hand and we walked briskly to the meetinghouse. We found a place and sat down. I placed the stool in front of me and surveyed the room. There was something obvious about everyone in that room. Like Mi-andee, they were all wearing the opposition party uniform and that made me instantly forgive my grandmother, even though I still did not understand what she was up to. The incident with Uncle was still very fresh in my mind, but I decided to let my confusion rest for a while. People were talking, sometimes loudly, sometimes quietly. People would turn around in their seats, observe the others in the room, and wave a greeting—tro-way salot—to the people they knew. There was a feverish air of expectation in the room. Once in a while, someone would "shshhhhhhh" and the talking would fade into subdued murmurs, but when no one appeared at the door, the conversation would resume and gain in intensity. A car suddenly came to an abrupt stop outside after what seemed to me like a year. We could all hear the screeching of tyres. The room was dead silent in a flash. I was surprised. I never thought adults could come to attention that quickly, as if they were school children. They were better than school children. Not one whisper in that room. The door opened and a group of old men dressed in party uniform filed through the door. Suddenly, everyone in the room was on their feet. Even my grandmother. The applause almost killed my eardrums. I couldn't see most of the people in front of or behind me but it looks as if my grandmother was the only one not clapping. She's an old woman. No one can hold it against her. The clapping died down, people slowly sat down and that's when I noticed the big man standing, his hands sticking out, almost weighed down by the voluminous folds of his boubou, as he moved them up and down beckoning the audience to quiet down. There were a few sporadic claps here and there . . .

> *Hip hip hip*, he bellowed.
> *Hurrah!*
> *hip hip*
> *hurraaaah*, came the thunderous response.
> And then the man began to talk.
> And then I fell asleep.

The applause in the room was deafening. I woke up. I didn't know how long I had been sleeping. Neither did I care. I noticed my grandmother firmly tying what looked like a couple of bills inside one of the ends of her wrappa. The party meeting was over and it was time to go home. We left the hall and walked straight to the compound we had "visited" earlier. Mi-andee ducked behind the house and reappeared her old self, wearing the PP Women's Wing uniform she had worn when we left home. We were now on our way to her subsection quarter meeting, she announced matter-of-factly.

"Mi?"

"Eh."

"Mi-andee?"

"Yes, my child. What is it?"

"How much money did those men give you?" I asked, tugging gently at her left hand.

"Fifty thousand," she said, winking at me.

It's when my grandmother says something like this that I know she really loves me. I knew she was lying. I never thought my grandmother could lie like that, in broad daylight, just to impress me. Who would give someone fifty thousand, fifty thousand francs! just so the person votes for their party. If any politician could do that, then our country must be full of crazy politicians. But I didn't dare share these thoughts with my grandmother.

We arrived at the house of the subsection president of the

Women's Wing in time for the kickoff of the meeting. Big Mami Grace, the president, has been my grandmother's friend for as long as I can remember. She gives a lot of party kickbacks to my grandmother that she does not give the other women. At least that's what my grandmother says. Mi-andee claims that besides their longstanding friendship, Mami Grace needs her as a political ally, what with her strong voice, her no-nonsense attitude, and especially her ability to rally women, to manipulate them into believing they were doing the right thing, working for the right party, voting for the right party, and so on and so forth. I suspect that Mami Grace gives these things to her friend because she knows Mi-andee can easily campaign against her and de-throne her. I knew all the women sitting in the room, so I walked around greeting everyone of them. They fondly re-turned my greeting, some rubbing my head, some pulling on my braids, some pinching my cheeks, others commenting on the size of my breasts, others stating that my grandmother will soon be harassing suitors coming to our compound to marry me . . . these women were all so funny. Imagine that. Me, getting married!

Mami Grace called the room to order. The women wasted no time. Party business was discussed and over with in no time. They allocated tasks, each woman volunteering to do one thing or the other, and they turned their attention to the three fifty-kilogram bags of parboiled, white, long-grain Pakistani rice their president was offering them. She thanked them for taking the time off their busy schedules to attend the party meeting. She thanked them for taking a stand against corruption and rotten politics. She applauded them for their strength, their will to fight for change, their courage to change the future for their children and grandchildren . . . Bottles of beer floated around the room as she spoke: "33" Export, a.k.a. kick-starter; Beaufort, a.k.a. jobajo; Satzenbräu; Guinness; and cans of Becks and St. Pauli Girl quietly but swiftly disappeared into the deep pockets of kaba ngondos . . .

"Long live our president," the women cooed, in between loud belches and gloogloo sounds of beer gushing down their gullets.

"Let's drink to her health."

"More grease to her elbows."

"May the ancestors multiply her blessings."

"May she continue to be our shining light."

"Ooh weh, ooh weh, oh weh oh weh oohhweeeeh."

"Wulililililililili iiiih!"

"Wuh wuh wuuuuuh!"

The bags of rice were emptied into a huge basin. One woman stood up. She undid and rewrapped her wrappa firmly around her waist. The women had all come prepared, for when the rice-sharer rose from her seat, empty salt bags appeared as if from nowhere. My grandmother unzipped her handbag and her own bag appeared too. It was like magic! The rice-sharer proceeded to give each member in the room an equal share. The women drank and talked, mostly about rival parties and about cheating husbands who ran after shameless married women and those girls they called ashawo. (This caused a lot of laughter from the group. What was so funny about married men running around? About calling young girls prostitutes?) Another woman walked round the room giving each woman a couple of bills. When she came to my grandmother's side, Mi-andee was listening intently to something Mami Grace was saying. Strange, I thought. I kept staring at the side of her face. She finally noticed, turned around, looked at me, pulled her lips together as if about to whistle, and pointed them at the hand of the money-sharer. I looked at the woman and opened my hand. My palm was a bit sweaty. I was excited. I was holding my grandmother's money in my hand. I looked at her face, but she was not looking at me. She had turned her attention back to the president. I couldn't help myself. I opened my palm and looked at the money. "This has to be three thousand francs," I tried to convince myself as I carefully spread out the bills. My eyes were popping out of my head. There were three ten-thousand franc bills sitting in the palms of my sweaty hands. I felt as if my heart had stopped beating. I was thinking to myself that politics must be a good thing if it can make women like Mami Grace so rich! I was thinking how I would like to become a politician and be rich like Mami Grace so I could give money to my friends. I knew the first person I would give money to would be Uncle Alienze—that way, people would stop laughing at him behind his back; that way, Auntie Maggie would smile more often when he is around. That way . . . I felt my grandmother's hand tugging at my hand. She pried the money out of my palms and the new bills took their place with the other notes. The meeting was over. I carried the rice on my head and the stool in my right hand and we headed home after saying our good-byes.

That evening I was sitting in the parlour with other children as we watched *Amen* followed by *The Fresh Prince of Bel-Air* on CRTV. *Party News* came on following these American shows. We had no interest in party news but the adults liked to watch so as to see the faces of their rivals in other opposition parties and comment on what "nonsense" they had to say. Most of them didn't get to see themselves or their party leaders on television. A law had been passed giving air time only to those few parties that were represented in the National Assembly. DP, the ruling party, got the lion's share. When the face of the president of one of DP's youth sections appeared on the screen, the children all sighed and most of them left our house—after all, they had only come to watch Thelma, Deacon Frye, Carleton, and Hillary. The adults immediately started hurling insults at the DP youth section president.

"Imagine!" my father cursed. "Look at what these people are doing. Look at where we are. Children who are still learning to clean their shit-hole are now talking at us, on my television . . . this television for which heavy lumps of my miserly salary are being deducted each month . . . without my consent . . . national television they say, and I don't have the right, my party doesn't have to right to use it because we're in the opposition, the real opposition, mind you! The true opposition that has refused to sell its soul to DP for a few seats in the assembly and the cabinet . . . those traitors . . . how dare they give DP a coalition? . . . How dare they? I ask you . . ."

This is how it always begins. Someone says something, someone sees a face on television, someone says something on the radio, and boom, everything is patapouf. The arguments about politics, the opposition, the ruling party, . . . gain momentum like an overflowing river, thundering swiftly down the hills in the rainy season, sweeping along everything in its path. The arguments get so heated, voices screaming so much, that no one seem to be hearing the other, nor do they particularly seem to care. You should hear them: oh, corruption eh; oh, cowardice eh; oh, hatred; oh, talk about killing someone; oh, talk about the state of emergency that is never going away; oh, talk about children under ten who instead of going to school to learn-book are becoming instead experts at making bombs with petrol, sand, and beer bottles; oh, talk about their children fighting army helicopters and tear gas; oh, much talk about killing the president, chopping off the heads of ministers, burning down the mansion of governors. Talk talk talk. CBP and its likes accusing everyone of rigging; PU accusing PP of rigging; PP accusing DP of rigging; everyone accusing DP of massive rigging, after all, DP has the guns, the bullies, everything—and so on and so forth. I could sense this was going to be a long night of senseless arguments, thanks to my father. Tsstsst, politics makes big people crazy. I gathered my things, as we say, and left the room. I had not walked five paces when I heard shouting.

Tegheh kwu! Not again.

"Weeh, wunna look. A beg wunna quiet. Big Mami dey for television. Big Mami dey for CRTV!"

"Wusai yi dey? Wusai e dey?" someone was asking, a tone of urgency in his voice.

"Na e dat. You no di see? Na yi dat. Or na blind you don blind. Na your mami dat . . ."

"Oh papa god eh. Oh papa god eh! Ooh ma mami eeeh! Na which kana baluck dis now? Weeeeeheeeeeeeh, na which kana baluck dis eeeeeeeeeh!"

"Who has died?" I thought to myself, my heart pounding as I turned around to retrace my steps.

I ran into the room just as my father was saying "witch woman" through clenched teeth. Half the eyes in the room were staring at my grandmother. If looks could kill, the stunned disbelief in their eyes, on their faces, would have snuffed the life out of her chest. Luckily for my grandmother, life in that room was playing everyone a dirty trick but herself. She was sitting on her favourite stool, her back against the wall, a bottle of "33" Export in her hands. She was sleeping peacefully, snoring as her head moved from side to side, the trente-trois bottle firmly in her grip. I watched her. I watched as her head moved to the left, stopped, made a semicircle swinging to the right, then jerked right back to the centre of her chest. The thick silence, heavy like ngo'o, seemed to startle her like a hungry child rousing from a hot afternoon slumber. She appeared to wake up. She looked sluggishly around, mouthed a "na weti eeh?" to no one in particular, took a long swig at the bottle, and as her hand came down from her mouth, she went right back to sleep, snoring the night away. My eyes reluctantly moved away from my grandmother's feeble, relaxed body and I turned my gaze to the television set, and there, boldly displayed on the screen for everyone to see, was the image of my grandmother. She looked beautiful, her head expertly wrapped in a colourful scarf, her teeth playfully smiling into the camera, her left hand tugging something underneath her blouse just below her left breast. Mi-andee looked beautiful, almost like a queen, in her DP uniform.

6

American Lottery

I

Paul's friends convened at their usual meeting venue and to-gether descended on his house. They invaded his tiny room, the room his aunt had given him to live in after he earned a maîtrise from the university and had not been able to find a "suitable" job. He had been languishing in this place for two years, he often said, doing one odd job after another, always hopeful about the future. A future that took the shape of going to America, everyday invading his needs, dreams, fantasies, nightmares . . . If not America directly, then America via Italy or Germany would be acceptable too. Unfortunately, the connection through Rome was getting more difficult to map out. The Germans were said to be nice, but difficult. Difficult yes, but at the same time, generous to a lucky few. So Germany could be an acceptable transit choice. Or the Netherlands? Or Norway? Not many people knew about the opportunities that lay there waiting. Norwegians were said to be so nice. But then it was so cold, just like Canada. But one could survive the

Canadian winter so long as it remained a Gateway to America. Had they not heard on their radios that the United Nations had voted Canada the best place in the world to live? But lately they had also been hearing stories about some of their compatriots locked up at Canadian borders. And another thing, he had no interest in dealing with the Anglo-French situation in Canada. It would remind him too much of the situation in Cameroon. Not something he needed in his life at the moment. He wanted to move forward. England? Only if worse came to the worst. England had become too old-fashioned for his tastes. England was, had been, HOME to his aunts, mothers, fathers, uncles—in short, his parents' generation. He got tired of hearing them enthuse about going HOME to London and their francophone counterparts, going HOME to Paris, to mbenge. He was fed up hearing about how white people really know how to build their countries. "What are we black people of Africa really doing that we can't even try to build a little bit like these white people," he would hear them ask scornfully. "Of course they had to—and still do—plunder all that we have to build their heavens," they would add unenthusiastically. Paul would listen with disgust as all the blame and anger was vented at the White Thief. England, that so-called mother country was not for him. And France? ABSOLUTELY, CATEGOR-ICALLY, UNEQUIVOCALLY . . . NOT. Underline NOT. Over his dead body. Absolutely, categorically, and unequivocally, *not*.

Paul saw himself as one of the increasing number of young Cameroonians from the minority English-speaking popula-tion whose hatred for THE enemy was almost visceral. For this strong, ambitious, intelligent, energetic young man, the France of the de Gaulles, the d'Estaings, the Chiracs, the france they had nicknamed les specialistes du provisoire, this france was the devil incarnate. france? Worse than the Ger-mans, worse than the British, who had all dominated and shared in the spoils of his country. france was the unspeakable.

The enemy within. The enemy to be crushed. france made him puke. Four years at the university, the carefully crafted institution of so-called national reconciliation and integration had only helped cement his view that the anglophones, who in their shortsightedness had chosen to stay with the crazy "Frogs," existed only to be dominated, exploited, and treated like underdogs, like second class citizens, by the majority francophone population—this under the auspices of the devil himself. No, America was the place to be . . . He needed to go away to a place where murderous thoughts would not be invading his everyday dreams . . . to a place where he would stop feeling, thinking, or believing that secession was the only option open to a minority . . .

Paul was still ruminating, mulling over and over in his mind, "America is the right choice. America . . . ," when his friends pushed the door open and breezed in without knocking. He was lying on his bed, wearing only his pants, the right side of which had glided up and was caught in the sacral area, exposing one bare buttock. A lone fly, perched on his ebony black skin, was boldly dusting off its wings and legs. George gave the exposed skin a loud smack. The insect noisily took flight, furious at the intrusion, and Paul's friends exploded in laughter, slapping each other on the back. Caught by surprise, Paul sprang from his bed like a tiger, the scowl of a lion on his face as he hurriedly put on a pair of trousers. Then they all sat down, two of the young men grabbing the two available chairs in the room while the other four sat on his bed. Paul apologised. He had no drinks to offer them, but George came to his rescue with 300 francs for the purchase of four litres of palm-wine. Chrisopher took the money, walked to the off-licence around the corner, and was back in no time. The friends drank and talked.

"Massa, so we hear you're going to America?"

That was George.

Paul smiled shyly.

"Massa, who's spreading such news?" he asked.

"Eh, boh, you know you can't lie to us. We're your friends. John, the postman, told us. He brought the good news yesterday from Douala himself."

"Yes, yours truly saw Sister Eli, who gave me the message, and I . . . ," he made a deep bow, and the others applauded. "I personally brought the message to His Royal Highness myself."

"Oh, John, stop it. Why are you doing this na, massa? I'm not going . . . yet."

"Yes, not yet, but you'll be going soon. Wuuh, just imagine, one of us is actually taking off for America sometime soon. Man, some people were born under bright stars and a full moon."

"Well, even if I do go . . . it won't happen that soon anyway," Paul blurted out.

"Liar. What do you think we are? A bunch of dunces?"

"Heh, do I detect some jealousy here?"

That was George again.

Paul fidgeted uneasily and poured himself another glass of palmwine.

"Heh, man, we're here to celebrate your good fortune with you. Why are you so glum?"

That was Christopher.

Paul forced a smile, switched personas, and calmly slipped back into the spirit of merriment. He smiled, he chuckled, he commented on not fully grasping the prospect of actually going to America looming so close by. It felt like a dream, an exciting dream. An uneasy dream.

"You don't have to feel uneasy about it, after all, this journey has consumed your life for the past three years . . . Remember those nights at the university when we would curse the Frogs, make flimsy though elaborate plans about going to

Europe or America and then go out and get plastered with "33" Export?

That was Linus.

They all laughed.

How could they not remember? They had been angry young men, angry at a system they claimed stifled their progress, crushed their hopes, and tried to usurp their identities. But they had not been prepared to give up what made them anglophone Cameroonians. They were a powerful minority to be reckoned with, they told themselves. They were going to fight tooth and nail. They were going to fight to the last drop of their blood . . . of their breath. They were going to change the world . . . their world. They were going to teach the Frogs an unforgettable lesson. They were going to . . . Oh, they remembered. It was just like yesterday!

"While you are laughing and downing cup after cup of this precious mbu'uh . . ."

That was Peter. Another explosion of laughter greeted his words.

"Yeh, man, this a real mbu'uh . . . I should start a company to bottle this white stuff . . ."

More laughter echoed in the room.

"Linus, while you were dreaming about your Palmwine Bottling Company, I was trying to say to my friend here that he has every reason to be uneasy about going to America. Actually, he should be afraid of going to America. America is a bad place . . ."

"Worse than france?"

Peter shot Linus one of his killer looks.

The young men all knew how Peter felt about America. He hated America as much as he hated France. But it was a hatred that had planted itself like a black jigga and had unobtrusively found nourishment in his flesh. If he had one goal in life, it was to travel the world the day he would strike it rich. He had even had dreams of one day travelling to America. Then his brother who had left for America when he was barely ten had come home for the first time after thirteen years, THIRTEEN YEARS! and bored holes, like those left behind on plantain leaves after the passage of hailstones, in his perception of America and the world. His brother had shattered a dream, a child's dream. His brother had come back a different person, a stranger: the way he walked; the way he smiled, the way he smiled at people; the way he talked, the way he talked to people; the way he ate, what he ate, when he ate; the way he dressed, what he wore . . . Who was this person? Peter had wondered.

"You know something, Linus, I don't want to compare those two countries but I do want to warn our friend. You saw what happened to my brother . . ."

The others sighed.

They rolled their eyes.

They punctuated both actions with, "Yeh, yeh, my brother, we know."

"You know something?" Peter asked in a grave voice, a voice that seemed to come straight out of his grandfather's grave. The friends were suddenly alert. This voice spelled one word: t-r-o-u-b-l-e, its language often pregnant like the growl of the kwefo.

"Paul, you have to be very careful. I don't envy you. You'll go to America, they'll treat you like dirt—no, they'll treat you like doti, yes, exactly, they'll treat you like what we say in Pidgin English, d-o-t-i! and instead of coming back home, you'll remain there like my *brother*, rot, and fertilise their crops."

"Americans told you they need Paul's cranky good-for-nothing carcass to fertilise their crops?"

Thunderous outbursts of laughter shook the room.

"Peter, why are you saying such horrible things?"

That was Athansius. He had not spoken since they sat down to drink. Years ago, the group had nicknamed him Quiet Hurricane. They claimed his words knew the depths from which a hurricane gathers its strength.

"America isn't such a bad place. Every child in this country dreams of going there . . ."

"CORRECTION," Peter hissed, almost jumping out of his chair.

"Alright, many young people, not only in this country but all over the world, dream of going to America, so what's so wrong with that?"

"The question is not, What's so wrong with that, but Why is that so?," Peter countered.

"What do you mean, Why is that so? It's easy. That's all the children see in the movies, in *Dallas, Dynasty, Santa Barbara,* in *The Fresh Prince of Bel-Air, The Cosby Show.* . . . Hell, the richest quartier in our capital city is now popularly called Santa Barbara. Give some taxi drivers the true-true name of that quartier and they have no idea what you're talking about. But when you finally say Santa Barbara some look at you (you can taste the scorn in their mouths) and bluntly ask why you didn't say so in the first place. Who remembers the indigenous name of that plush residential area? You lived in the capital for four years. Do you?"

"My point exactly," Peter said with a calm that frightened even his friends.

There was a suppressed calm that was bitter, almost poisonous. It spread like a thick fog, smearing dark shadows on their faces. It spoke of the anger, frustration, and disillusionment that the young men sitting in the room shared. It sat sour, slimy, like stale food in their mouths.

"That's exactly what America does. It exports the *'good'* side of itself and you spend the good years of your life dreaming of becoming a carefree Marlboro cowboy, you dream of going to America and becoming the best friend of the Carringtons, to whom you'll proudly show exotic Africa . . .

Then you go there and they tell you you're just a black man, you're just a *person-of-color*, you're just . . ."

"Heh, Peter, wait wait wait . . . wait a minute. What's this thing about a person who has colour? What's a person of colour? Don't we all have colour? Do white people not have colour, or am I just blind?"

"Not to white people they don't. *White* doesn't seem to be a colour. From what my brother says, white people think they're colourless, transparent, . . ."

"Uuuuuuuuuugh! *Transparent?*" the others loudly chorused.

"How can a person be colourless? . . . Close your eyes. Picture looking at a person who is without colour. Un-coloured! Ugh, that's ugly. I don't want to see what's inside that transparent person. I might have nightmares . . ."

The others did not let George finish. They were all talking over their heads. Look, a colourless person, went Christopher's high pitched whistle. Hmm, a transparent person! John wriggled his nose. Who in God's name had such an insane idea? Linus swore. The whole thing sounded crazy to them. Some chuckled, some laughed, until Peter's baritone, like the quiet persistent rumble of the midnight drum, jolted them back to reality.

"Well, my brother says that white people sat down and put it in their heads that anything that has a colour, like our black skin, contaminates everything else, giving it a different colour . . ."

"So what? Isn't that a good thing? Black, creating multiple colours?"

"Quiet Hurricane, you don't understand . . ."

"What's there not to understand . . . ?"

"Well, my brother says that in America . . ."

"Yes, yes, yes! Your brother this, your brother that . . ."

"Listen, let me tell you something. In America, white people pretend not to see you, you are invisible to them, or when they do see you, they only see your skin and they blame every-thing wrong in America on your skin. That's how they eat you up . . . Like my brother."

"Are you sure your brother's telling the truth?"

"What do you think? Even if he is exaggerating, there must be a lot of truth to what he says. There's no smoke without fire."

"True, but your brother's experience might be unique. He could also be paranoid . . ."

"I scrutinised my brother when he was here. I watched him, I followed him around, I listened to him. He regaled us with a lot of stories but it was only when he discussed this matter that his eyes clouded over. He looked so helpless, frightened, like a little child. Sometimes he even cried, but we couldn't help him because we didn't understand this thing he was talk-ing about. We heard him, but we didn't understand."

"Why are you so bitter about something you don't under-stand?"

"I could see through my brother. I tried to imagine what this monster is that breaks a grown man like that and I still can't."

"This is funny. In this country, do we really care about see-ing or not seeing white people? We Cameroonians see Bamilekes, we see Ewondos, Bassas, Magidas, Douala people, Bamenda people, Bakwerians, Bayanges, et cetera. Perhaps in a rural area some people might, out of sheer curiosity, run out to see what a 'white' person physically looks like. I mean, we only think of white people (if they have any meaning in our lives, when we think of the dear old Mother Country and La Belle France, not forgetting that America has joined in the dance), of how they're pulling the strings of this damned government of ours, which will continue to be neocolonial until we crush it ourselves . . . And don't tell me I'm a dreamer. Who cares about a 'white' person in this country? In this country where they don't even look white oo! I don't know what your 'white' people in America are talking about! Do you know what a 'white' person is called in my language? A 'white' person is called, word for word, person-that-is-red, red-person. And they think they have no colour! Now, let's think about this for a minute . . . imagine you go there and tell a 'white' person that they're not really white but red, like an unripe plum. What do you think they'll say to you?"

"I think the person will just pull out their gun and, pam pam, blast your black brains to hell . . ."

The laughter was deafening. The boys guffawed as they had not all evening.

"Well, I really don't care. You can philosophise all you want. Person-of-colour has no meaning for me. Look, I am African, I am Cameroonian. End of discussion. Let's shelve this thing. That's their problem. Let them deal with it. Paul will deal with it when he gets there. After all, how have the others survived there? . . . I move we discuss our plan of action for Wednesday."

They agreed it was time to connect with their local reality, with the other burning issues, especially the upcoming strike and Civil Disobedience rally that was being planned for Friday of the following week. Paul felt a tinge of guilt tug at his heart. He was having regrets about missing these struggles for democracy that his people had fervently embraced, prepared to spill to the last drop of blood in their veins. He was feeling nostalgic about the riots, the curfews, the strikes, the rallies; even the hysteria that like cerebral malaria sometimes whipped the crowds into a frenzy; the never-ending tug of war with the government. And the deaths. The martyrs who were dying for something that was real, tangible, but oh-so-fleeting; martyrs, who were dying to save and restore their collective soul, their ancestral heritage. Why was he leaving behind this unique opportunity to be a part of historic events that would bring true democratic change for his people? Why was he fleeing all this for a place that seemed to be oh-so-fleeting. Why was he abandoning the devil he knew for the angel he did not know? Could Peter be right? Or was he just a bitter young man who had seen himself betrayed by a reckless older brother?

II

This entire humbug began rather innocently, the day before. Paul was walking with his usual swagger, his dark, lanky body gliding through the motor-park as if he had no worry in the world. His left hand rested casually in the left pocket of his trousers in such a way that his elbow was raised at an approximate forty-five-degree angle, slightly raising his left shoulder. The tilt, from left to right, seemed to enable him to walk with total ease, bending his knees with regular strides, weaving his wiry build in and out of the groups of people in the crowded park. Effortlessly. Leisurely. His gait betrayed no haste. Occasionally, he recognised someone and raised his right hand for a firm, short handshake, the smile glued to his face, amusement dancing in his eyes.

He was pursuing this aimless walk when he heard his name. The voice seemed to be coming from the back of his head, so he had to turn around. He pivoted on his heels, straining his eyes and ears, his left hand still securely lodged in his pocket.

"Paul, Paul, this way, this way," a young man was shouting, frantically waiving his right hand, his head sticking through the window of a moving bus.

"Paul, na me eh. Na me John ah di call you . . . Paul, look for dis side no you too . . . for this side!"

The voice seemed to be floating to him from the section of the park where Douala vehicles off-loaded their passengers.

He instinctively walked in that direction. Then he saw a hand waving at him and recognised John's boyish face.

"Eh boh, na you?"

"Eheh na me eh," John replied.

"So massa, wusai you commot now?"

"Massa, ah be just run go Douala dis morning . . ."

"And you don already come back now now so? Welcome oo."

"Thank you."

They had been talking to each other through an open window as Paul awaited his friend's turn to get off the bus. The instant his feet touched the ground, they shared a firm, long handshake, their left hands clasped behind each other's back. They continued to shake hands vigorously, talking, laughing, drumming on each other's back with their fingers. Then they slid their hands down the length of their arms, bringing them together, forming a fist for one last friendly grip, their foreheads almost touching, the laughter still on their lips. It had taken them a little while to get through their greeting ritual and to finally let go of each other's hands.

"So what took you to Douala now, massa?" Paul asked his friend as they manoeuvred their way out of the motor-park, pushing through throngs of busy, loud-talking folk.

"Boh, I went there to take care of some small business."

"What kind of business now, massa?"

"I went to see that Ibo man . . . Remember, I told you I wanted to do some petty trading between Cameroon and Nigeria . . . ?"

"Yes, I remember . . . but massa, you want to go into business with an Ibo man . . . ?"

"Paul, my brother, one has to survive oo."

"Yes, but with these Nigerians, one can never be too careful oh, my brother. Look, they've taken over our economy here in the southwest . . . in the northwest . . . They're everywhere, in Douala, Yaoundé . . . They own entire quartiers in our towns, everywhere . . ."

"Massa, I hear what you're saying, but times are hard and one has to survive . . . and by the way, they don't own everything. So stop exaggerating this thing about the Nigerian invasion . . ."

"Yeah," Paul concurred, looking pensive. "Yes, we've got to survive."

"Uh-huh."

"So, what's this business venture?"

"Well, I want to go into the business of selling eru . . ."

"Wuuh, you really mean it?"

"Yes I do. Look at all the eru that leaves this country, this town, for Nigeria everyday, every single day. I mean, the Idenau road is so busy nowadays. Haven't you noticed? . . . Tuesdays, Thursdays, and Saturdays are the busiest."

"Yes, my friend. There are more police check points now on this little stretch of road than there've ever been . . . just so the police can extort money from all the people exporting eru and other foods to Nigeria."

"And from those importing funge, federal, zoa zoa, whatever you want to call it. After all, our cars need the cheap petrol to run in these times of economic crises . . ."

"Coupled, tripled, no, quadrupled with the devaluation of the almighty CFA franc . . ."

"Please, Paul, I'm in a good mood today. So don't, I repeat, do not take me down the CFA road . . . fifty percent devaluation, seventy percent salary reductions . . . that's why we deserve the title, the third world . . . Anyway, as I was saying . . . About zoa zoa. I was going to say it's funny that we produce top-quality petrol in this country but are forced to buy cheap fuel from Nigeria. And Nigerians themselves have to queue in long lines at petrol stations and sometimes have to go on strike because of fuel shortages! In a petroleum-producing country! Ironic, isn't it? This is *post*-colonial Africa. Survival of the fittest, or may I say, survival of the richest? Anyway, their loss is our gain. It's survival, alright . . . All this trading and trafficking between Idenau and Nigeria has only given the police more ways to make fast money . . ."

"Yah, especially the trafficking. Black market always pays."

"What with all the cheating and the chaos that surrounds us, the black market must flourish but sometimes it takes you six feet deep!" John replied, theatrically drawing a coffin in the air with his hands.

The young men both shared a warm, intoxicating laugh. In their postcolonial context of daily uncertainties, laughter was the vitamin they consumed for daily strength. It cloaked their sarcasm, their frustrations; it buried their anger three feet deep, where it lay smouldering like hot food wrapped in plantain leaves.

"How are you going to find the eru?" Paul asked, looking skeptically at his friend. "You're not going to go to the forests yourself, are you?"

"Oh, no," John replied. "I did a lot of eru hunting when I was young. What I want to do is go to the villages or bush-markets and buy the eru directly from the women who harvest it . . . The advantage is, I know most of them."

"I'm sure you do. All those women must have babysat you when you were young . . ."

"Yes, my friend. You know how it is in the village. You're never only your mother's child."

"So what you're saying is, you want to become a bayam-sellam?"

"Exactly. I'll go to the village, buy from the women and then bring my bales of eru here and sell to the Ibo man, who will then export it to Nigerian markets. I like this bayam-sellam idea."

"Yah, it's a good plan. But you have to be careful with these

Ibos. They're leeches. They'll suck your blood dry, so, you have to be very careful . . ."

"Don't worry, my blood is not that tasty. And you forget, it's business. Leeching is the foundation of capitalism, you take it or leave it . . ."

"My friend, I'm surprised at you . . ."

"Hmm. You ought to leave that dream world of yours and join us in the Real World. The good thing is my cousin Joe has a Toyota pickup and has agreed to transport the eru from the villages to town . . . at a good price, of course."

"Now you're talking. So how is Joe anyway?"

"Oh, the man is surviving . . . What can I say? . . . I also brought him a message from that his Bami woman, so I have to go to his place when I'm done with you . . ."

"Heh, you mean to tell me Joe is still swinging with that Bamileke chick?"

"Uh-huh."

"I thought his mother hates the girl . . ."

"So? Ah, Joe doesn't care. He told his mother he loves the woman, Bami or no Bami. What's the girl's tribe got to do with anything . . . ?"

The two friends guffawed knowingly. They were both dating "outsiders." They were amused by how dating outside one's tribe can sometimes cause bitter rifts between children and parents.

"By the way, I brought a message for you from your sister . . ."

"Ah-hah, I knew something was cooking. Which sister?"

"The one who lives in New Bell."

"Really, you went to New Bell?"

"No, she was at the motor-park looking for someone who could take the message to you."

"Luckily you were there."

"Uh-huh."

"So, what is it?"

"She says she received a form from America for you . . . and you need to come for it at once."

"A form? What form?"

"She didn't explain. She said someone, or your brother . . . I don't remember exactly . . . faxed it to your uncle's office and then someone brought it to her house . . . Something about going to America . . . I think."

Paul looked pensive. Almost troubled. His body suddenly went limp, cold. He could feel goose pimples popping up all over his skin. Then an unexplainable wave of heat engulfed his body. His back muscles and thighs contracted, trembled as if synchronised to respond to a dance call. His heart was roaring in his chest. He was afraid John could hear it beating loudly, like a ceremonial drum warming up and beckoning the village to an august funeral celebration. He could feel a warm wetness collecting into a pool at the base of his neck and cascading down the hollow of his spine. He could hear the echoes raging like buffaloes through his chest. This was it! It was finally happening! . . . But not yet. Not while John's probing stare drilled holes through his face.

"I wonder . . . I wonder why it's so urgent," Paul said almost casually, sticking both hands into his pockets. He let his body rock to the rhythm of his heart as he continually raised his heels, just a millimetre every few seconds, his ten toes firmly planted on the ground.

"Well, you're probably finally leaving for America . . . that's what you've wanted for a . . ."

"Still, I wonder . . ."

"Stop wondering and go to Douala . . . and when you return, do let me know when we can have the going away party . . ."

"Massa, stop joking like that . . ."

"I've told you and I'll tell you again, it's survival . . ."

"Alright massa. I'll keep you posted when I get back."

They shook hands, clasped each other on the shoulder for a long embrace, shook hands again, and promised to keep in touch with the news about going to America. John walked away murmuring, "survival, man, survival," an almost cynical smile on his face. The second his back turned the corner, Paul took off like an arrow. As is the custom with his people, he asked his feet whether he had ever eaten and forgotten to share his food with them. And as his people would say, his feet responded, "Never." And so he ran. He ran as he had not in a long, long time, his feet anxiously catapulting his every step. He was darting through the streets, as if he had springs glued to the soles of his feet. He had to see his aunt immediately. He needed to borrow a thousand francs for his transport fare to Douala.

III

And the rest is history, as they say. The news about Paul's impending departure to the United States of America spread like wildfire. Rumours have a way of spreading faster than truth in these parts. Sleek, like hot flames, they disseminate their warmth and quietly but surely roast up everything in their wake. We love our rumours. Too often, they are sweeter and juicier than real life. We love our rumour machine, the one we Cameroonians call radio trottoir, for often we really do not care whether the stories are true. What is truth anyway? How does truth fit into our lives, in this landscape polluted by convoluted politics? Can there be truth in a world that the powers-that-be have infused with cunning, greed, disillusionment, . . . ah, you complete the list. Yes, we love our rumours. They are the tidbits that now spice up our lives, lubricating, soothing our aching bones like engine oil on sturdy pistons.

Parties—farewell parties, celebration parties—were being held for Paul, my little brother, by relatives and friends all over: near, far, and wide. America! their own son, their own friend, their kinsman was going to America. The frenzy, the joy. Imagine! He will soon be rolling in dollars, their tongues wagged. The very bed on which he will lie will be made of dollars, they chanted. Soon, we will receive pictures showing him standing tall, regal, all-African, smiling with his hand on the hood of his huge American car, fondly caressing it. Soon we will receive pictures showing him standing in front of his huge American house. Soon, we will receive pictures taken with his brothers and sisters: Cameroonians, Nigerians, Ethiopians, Eritreans, Egyptians, Black South Africans, Kenyans, Senegalese, pictures with some Black Americans, and of course, a picture with the inscription on the back that simply says, "a friend"—a white woman, her hand around his waist as they both laugh and show their teeth to the camera. She will look so beautiful, almost too happy, as she holds firmly onto my little brother, our African son. And then the years will go by. And the parties will fade into bitter memories, figments of our imagination.

My brother borrowed the money from our aunt, came to Douala to see me, and picked up the fax Livinus had sent from America. It's been so long, such a long time. To the family, Livinus is dead, buried, forgotten. But he will not let us forget, for once in a blue moon Livinus does a crazy thing like this, a crazy thing that only destroys other people the same way he has destroyed himself. My uncle was furious, disgusted, when he received that fax. When our father died, he had singlehandedly, with his own sweat and out of the goodness of his heart, raised Livinus, sent him to school so that Livinus could one day help raise us, his siblings. That's how we do it. We are raised and we help raise others. It is the chain of responsibility that keeps us together as families. One hand washes the other.

Two hands, multiple hands, tie the bundle known as the family. But Livinus had other ideas. When he won that scholarship, my uncle almost didn't let him go. What about your siblings, my uncle had asked. But then he relented. It was a good opportunity. Livinus would be able to occupy a senior-level position in any company when he returned with an American MBA in two years. What's more, Livinus could be sending some money home while he pursued his degree. Others had done it. Why not Livinus? But that was too many years ago. That fax drove him into a fit, but my uncle has always been too respectful of others. That is his one flaw. That fax was Paul's and even though it came from a ghost in his past, my uncle made sure Paul got it. It was a "DV"-something. Some bogus thing about an American immigration lottery that would grant permanent residence to thousands of aliens! Who are aliens? Where do aliens come from? I ask myself. Most probably, from the land of the living dead. I tell you, only those people who have made my brother Livinus into such a being could have dreamed up such a label. Today I mourn because I have truly made my little brother into one of these aliens, one of those ghosts from the land of the dead . . .

Yes, I gave him the fax. "This paper is like an owl's wail," I told him. But Paul did not hid my warning. He did not listen to the hoot of the owl. He applied. Took the precious envelope to the post office to hand it personally to my friend Esther, who works there. There had been too many rumours about instructions handed down to postal workers by the Head of State himself, to withhold all DV-applications. "Let them leave for America only after the dateline for the receipt of applications," the order had allegedly stressed. How could Paul take a chance? He had to put all the odds in his favour. This was one lottery he had to win. And, as you can imagine, by now, the word *lottery* had conveniently disappeared from our rumour tidbits. Paul was becoming a Permanent Resident Alien of the

United States of America! He was only waiting for his file to be processed (you know how these consulates treat us) and he would be on his way!

Esther wasn't at her desk when Paul sauntered into the post office that morning, so he gave his precious envelope to our onetime friend Cordelia. You see, two years ago, Esther had "taken" Cordelia's man. He came in one day, at the end of the day's work to pick up Cordelia but "his woman" was in the ladies room, so he struck up a conversation with Esther. That man—a married man—was too much of a woman-wrappa. Esther hooked up with him and dumped him a few months later. But that isn't what matters. When Paul walked in that morning, he gave Cordelia the chance to exact revenge on Esther. She had not forgiven Esther all the material things—a huge refrigerator, a large piece of land, a trip with the sango to England, and of course the usual things like jewelry, clothes—that Esther got out of her short fling with her former concubine. These are things that women always remember but that men often forget. That was Paul's small mistake. Cordelia smiled sweetly at Paul and promised to give the envelope to Esther. She watched Paul walk jauntily through the door, pursed her lips, pulled open her drawer, and calmly placed the envelope with the rest of her files.

In the meantime, festivities kept pace with life in my little brother's name, in my small brother's honour. It's funny how people hunger for parties in these difficult times. Every excuse to share a cup of palmwine or a bottle of beer is voraciously welcomed, especially when someone else is offering. Paul was riding the clouds of the future. My poor mother heard the news. Her son was about to leave for America in five days . . . in five days! She dragged herself from the village, braving those treacherous roads, to come see her son, afraid he might leave without saying good-bye, afraid she was never going to set eyes on him again. How does a mother live with the loss of two sons? With the knowledge of two sons consumed by an alien land she couldn't conjure up in her mind, her thoughts? . . . But the days went by. Paul was still here. And the months dragged on. And Paul was still here. They dragged on, lazily, like the waters on a shallow river bed in the heart of the dry season. Paul was still here. And the day finally came. That fateful day when Cordelia had to go to the hospital before coming to work and Esther had to get the date stamp out of Cordelia's file cabinet. She pulled the drawer open, found the date stamp but just as she was about to close it, a name caught her eye: ABENYAM, Funye Paul, followed by an address neatly typed on the top left-hand corner of an envelope. We don't write our names and addresses on envelopes, let alone type them. Those are the ways of the whiteman that our been-to brothers and sisters use when they send us letters from abroad. Abenyam, Funye Paul. This must be important, Esther thought. This could only be Elizabeth's brother, my friend thought again to herself. Paul's twin brother, Chebe, had died at birth. What were the odds that another Paul Abenyam lived in their town, who was also a twin? The chances were slim. Esther picked up the envelope. Realisation struck and my friend could not hold back her scream . . .

Cordelia was viciously attacked the moment she walked through the door into their workplace. A vigorous fight ensued, right there in the office. Esther never gave her the time to put her handbag down. Earrings flew across tables. Flying high-heeled shoes caught bystanders by surprise. Invectives I cannot mouth here polluted the air. Like mad women, they went for each others throats. Rack, crack, c-r-a-c-k, r-a-c-k went their nails, ripping apart their clothes. It's a miracle they didn't pluck each other's eyes out (I must confess that onlookers stopped that from happening). The news spread. Like wildfire, the rumour spread. You've guessed it. Paul heard the news too . . .

The day you shall have the time or the chance to walk down Freedom Street, look carefully, just look at the corner of Freedom and Survival, you will see a tall, lanky, bearded old man, who sleeps under the shelter of the huge mango tree. That old man who talks to himself, staring into space, staring at the leaves, at the moon, talking with the stars, singing in the rain; that old man who shivers from the cold some nights, whose manhood lies bare for all the children to ogle, giggle at, and mock; for all the children who run by, some shouting, some screaming, some laughing; that old man they call Pa, or Popaul, or Papa Popaul; that old man is my little brother, Paul. I made him into an alien.

7

Accidents Are a Sideshow

It is the deep of night. The world is asleep. The owls are awakening. A young woman is in bed, caught in the throes of a recurring nightmare: She is leaving her house, very early in the morning, once a week as she does these days, and heading directly for "the embassy." There is already a long line of people waiting. She sighs, yet is grateful she made it that early. What's a two-hour wait? they are all asking each other. At least at this embassy, they didn't have to wait long hours only to make an appointment on when to return for a visa application form. A hand finally waves her in. She floats through the door, stands at attention, and waits for the security check. She opens her handbag. A man with cold, expressionless eyes dips his hands into the bag and methodically ploughs through its contents in a matter of seconds. He points to an open basket and she deposits her handbag in it. He waves her through metal detectors. She cringes and holds her breath. Her heart is racing, her palms are sweaty. She resists the temptation to wipe them on her dress. (A friend had jokingly told her one day that the metal detectors in this particular embassy were used for something other than security . . . they were used to slowly erase the memories of all those seeking visas to go to their country. Manda had taken the joke seriously. Framing her body within the confines of those cold rectangular metals always made her flinch. She always took a deep breath, blanking out everything she knew before stepping through. She could then retrieve her memories on the other side.)

She crosses the two-inch bridge and is now on the other side. She takes in a deep breath. Smiles. Her memories are intact. She is handed an application form. She fills it out, tenders it to the man who is also requesting the ten- or twelve-thousand-franc (the ever-fluctuating equivalent of twenty dollars), nonrefundable application fee. She sits and waits. She waits. She waits. Names are being called from the window up there. She can hardly see the faces spitting out those names. She looks up, directly at the cubicle, and catches the glimpse of a man, young, handsome and a woman, middle-aged, plain, with a very noticeable freckled nose. Their voices are sharp, penetrating, judgmental. Theirs are voices of power, of ownership, of control. Another name. She waits. Finally, her turn. Her name is mispronounced. She almost misses it. Imagine that. She cannot afford to frown, so she walks briskly in the direction of the little rectangular window. She hears a man's voice. So you want to go to the United States . . . It is a statement. Not a question. Why? he asks. She looks up through the cubicle. No face. She steps back two steps. The face of the young man is in full view. She looks at his eyes. They say nothing. She can feel herself readjusting her pose, bending her head, looking down at her feet. Her mind is floating away. The young man is talking. She cannot remember why she is here . . . When you have all of those documents, you can come back, but not before . . . She is walking through the metal detectors. She does not remember to hold her breath.

She is back. Again. Her used manila envelope in her hand. It is sweat stained and creased on all corners. It has had a rough

life but has also handled her documents with care. She is going
through the motions in her mind, rehearsing . . .
go through security check
open handbag
put open handbag here
Take a deep breath.
walk through metal detectors, there,
pick up handbag
hold manila envelope firmly
walk through door
Take a deep breath.
look up, look down
remove documents from envelope
look up
place documents, up, up in little cubicle
sit down and wait
Name called.
stand up, walk to window,
look up, up!
Papers shuffling. Where's this document? comes a squeaky
voice. It's in there. Where's this, where's that? Shuffle, shuffle,
shuffle. Where's . . . ? It's, it's in that pile, that package.
(Raised blond eyebrows.) The, the one I gave you, the one I
put up there, up in the window. Shuffle, paper shuffle. Where's
this, where's that; where where where . . .

Her hand weighs ten tons, it can barely reach the pile of
sheets. The manila envelope opens. She can hear the papers
falling inside like rocks on a cement floor. Her handbag
weighs ten tons. It hangs limply down her side. She cannot
feel her feet. She drags them through metal detectors, passed
glass-eyed security guards. She is out in the sun. The rays are
burning through her eyelids. The voice is drumming through
her head: bring more letters. We need to see more letters,
bring more letters, proof he is your husband. Preferably letters with the envelopes in which they arrived. With the

address of the sender and the canceled postage stamp with date, with, with with with . . .

"Jesus!" Manda swore. She realised she was absentminded when her car narrowly missed hitting one of the cigarette bill-boards that stood imposingly along the streets. She particularly disliked this billboard. The picture showed a man, well at ease, dressed in an expensive suit and tie, his coat nonchalantly swung over his shoulder, barely hanging onto the tips of his left middle and forefingers. In his right hand was a cigarette. He was smoking, in a carefree manner. It almost gave the impression the cigarette wasn't there. Almost an illusion. Then there was the woman, clutching his right elbow, smiling all the way. There was nothing in the world to worry about. About a hundred metres away was another billboard with yet another well-dressed male, walking as if he had not the slightest concern with the world around him. What was there to fret about? An array of glittering skyscrapers towered over him in the background. Underneath was inscribed the slogan: The American Way of Life. He was not smoking. He was simply selling a dream that remained a fatal fantasy in the reality of the daily lives of the people he seemed to be smiling at. Tucked at the bottom left corner of the large poster was a cigarette packet, the last thing to be noticed. It was discreetly opened, exposing three vertically positioned butts that, one after the other, led down a staircase into the well below. Yet another billboard, strategically placed at the roundabout further up from her street, portrayed a woman, impeccably dressed; pearls graced her ears, all of her neck, from top to bottom, and her delicate wrists. She was puffing away, her head turned skywards, an intoxicating smile of satisfaction smeared across her seemingly ageless face. Her white teeth and manicured nails had a life all their own.

Manda heaved a heavy sigh. She had not wanted her day to

begin this way. First there was that horrible dream, a dream yes, but oh-so-familiar she could taste its stale after taste. A dream that had moved in and claimed one side of her bed. She wished she would stop having the dream. Why did this life have to crawl into the peacefulness of her sleep? Give it up, she would say to herself everyday she returned from the embassy. Just sit here and let the man finish his studies and return in five years. But how can I do that? her other voice would query. They wanted proof he was her husband, they wanted proof both had been married for a long time, they especially wanted proof she was going to return to Cameroon. A return ticket wasn't proof enough. Her job wasn't proof enough. What did they want? Her blood? Why did they think we all wanted to go and stay in their country? Manda was angry. She was past being frustrated. The rage in her was burning so fiercely she feared she might hurt someone. Why would getting a stupid visa to visit one's mate, friend, lover, or relative reduce a human being to a beggar, to nothing? She was not going to let them win. Never. But she knew she also had to do something about the bitterness that remained firmly logged in the pit of her throat. Later, she had thought. But then again, here she was, sitting in her car, her heart pounding at two hundred kilometres an hour, as her son would say, her angst burning holes through a cigarette billboard. When she left home this morning, she had tried to think as many positive thoughts as she could. Today, especially, she needed to make an extra effort. This had nothing to do with the nauseating smells they had learned in the past two years to tolerate and coexist with in their city. When this city was what it used to be, the streets were clean, the grass cut, the lawns immaculate. Most of all, the city was beautiful, with a simplicity that only mother nature possessed the secrets to. It was uplifting, often mesmerizing, to contemplate and admire this city that boasted an impressive array of undulating, unending hills and valleys. At night, when the lights came on, the city looked almost ferric. All you had to do was position yourself on a hill top and let your gaze play cat and mouse with the view, taking in the breathtaking colours, the curves of hills and valleys intertwining, complementing each other. An aerial view was even more enchanting. The shadows undulated and the lights blinked like a million shooting stars. Those were the days! Now, their city looks like one huge garbage dump and smells like the intestines of rotten fish. Garbage has become an intrinsic part of their paysage, and an intricate part of their lives. Most of the streets in residential areas have become open-air graveyards where mounds of refuse are steadily laid to rest and forgotten. Often, the garbage pile gets so high that it cuts off traffic and an exasperated citizen decides to set fire to the refuse. This sacrificial burning clears up part of the road for cars to squeak through and more space for yet more garbage. Huge bales of grey and black smoke, like patient vultures, flap their wings lazily over the city. They decorate the skies like a canopy, creating a spectacle that far surpasses the one seen in villages right after an early evening rainfall (when little thin lines of smoke can be seen, bursting through thatched roofs, spiraling aimlessly towards the sky, enveloping the entire village). City folk no longer flinch at blocking their nostrils with their fingers. Who has any use for decency in this atmosphere of total decay? Either they hold their breath or they simply fan away the smoke and smells with their palms as they walk around, going about their daily business of survival. Manda was convinced that there must be a god somewhere looking out for them, for that alone could explain why there had not been any severe outbreaks of cholera. The last outbreak was barely forgotten, yet its comeback seemed so oppressively imminent. Mosquitoes were now everywhere in a city that not so long ago boasted of a drop in fevers and malaria epidemics. Typhoid fever and malaria were on the rise and in these days of CFA devaluation many could not afford the nivaquines and the quinimax.

Manda tried not to think about the filth that surrounded her and marred her mood every morning as she drove off to work. Every morning she said to herself, "I won't get angry today," but as soon as the ochre perfume of ruptured sewage pipes assaulted her nostrils, she knew the day would be a long one. At least she felt sheltered when she was indoors. She would shut her windows, draw her curtains, and mentally obliterate what she had just left outside. Now she had to face the outside. She cursed, ignored the stench, put the car in first gear, gave the billboard one last scornful look, and was on her way. There was no rush. The roads were equally bad. Potholes of all sizes were everywhere. Her grandfather, who once came from the village to visit, had shrewdly commented that some of the gullies on the roads swallowed up cars like a tasty lump of achu down a Beba man's throat. Grandfather had not returned for another visit. The few rides he had taken around the city had been enough. His back had hurt so much.

Manda tried to focus on her agenda for the day. But this was the long holiday period and groups of holiday makers could be seen everywhere on the streets. They invaded the roads with huge signs, strategically positioned, that read, MOTIVA-TION. While some of the boys dug up little amounts of earth by the roadside to fill up some of the holes, others stood with empty cans in their hands shaking them vigorously at the drivers, shouting, *"motivation, motivation!"* They all seemed to be more interested in the reward than the job they had elected to perform as good samaritans. When this youth "movement" emerged, as if out of the blue, to save the city's streets, city folk were quite generous with their fifty- and hundred-franc coins. The tin cans stuck through car windows rattled happily. But the drivers soon realised that the young men were on the streets to make a living, not shoulder the duties of the mayor.

Nowadays, some drivers would grudgingly drop coins but most drove by, pretending not to notice or simply sporting pronounced scowls on their faces. In this city you learned how to tune out smells and ignore streetwise kids ready to make some fast CFA. *"Maman, motivez! Motivez, maman,"* they screamed. Manda was thankful the tin cans had stopped rattling. She had to do a better job of tuning out their voices.

She drove on, oblivious to their screams and curses. She was on her way to "the consulate." She was dreading her trip to this consulate even more than her constant journeys to "the embassy." Midway through town, she stopped to pick up her cousin Manoji, whose neighbourhood boasted of fewer dumps. It had to. The centre of the town and all the routes that led to hotels and plush, select, residential areas had to maintain a semblance of sanity for those nonnatives who zoomed in and out of their city. North-south relations and politics had a face, one that, as with a drug, could not do without this constant cosmetic surgery. Manda watched as her cousin steamrolled his way to the car. Manoji never walked like normal human beings do. His steps literally seemed to bounce off each other and Manda always found this very amusing. Manoji jumped into the passenger seat and greeted his cousin.

"So how is it in New Jack City today?"

"Oh, the usual. And how is Dallas, I might venture to ask?"

"Oh, fine, just fine," Manoji replied. "I'll tell you something in confidence though. Lately, I have been thinking of moving to Santa Barbara."

Manda's laughter took Manoji by surprise.

"That must be the biggest joke I've heard this morning," she said, looking at her cousin, who did not seem amused in the least. "You're joking."

"No, I'm not," he replied seriously. "Why would you think that? You know I never joke when it comes to matters of comfort."

"What are you talking about?" Manda fired back. "You live in a nice little place, right now . . ."

"Little, yes, you just said it, little . . ."

"A really nice comfortable place," Manda continued, ignoring him. "And, and, right now you can barely make the rent . . ."

There, she said it. She expected a storm of words that never came. No raving, no ranting. Even Manoji surprised her this morning. He just chuckled and chuckled and chuckled. Manda was taken aback by this hearty display of mirth. Brutal reductions in salaries that had culminated with the final nail in the coffin—the devaluation of the CFA franc—had done strange things to her people. It had become a task all its own to distinguish genuine laughter from downright resignation and contempt. She waited patiently for her cousin to stop smirking.

"You know something my sister," Manoji cut into her thoughts. "Your problem in life has always been that you don't know how to seize the moment and live. I mean, live life. You're ever so cautious. Come to think of it, that must be why we love each other so much. Look, this place is totally rotten. People are completely miserable . . ."

"You don't look miserable to me!"

"Yes, that's why I have to move from Dallas to Santa Barbara. Yes, Santa Barbara, here I come . . . the most expensive residential area of our time . . . in this country . . . fweefwee."

"Stop whistling," Manda snapped, in spite of herself. She had promised herself to be patient with her cousin.

"I need more space, more clean air, more . . . Jesus, why should some people have it all and others nothing? Eh? You answer me that, why? I work hard like everyone else . . ."

Manda knew exactly where this conversation was going and she was not ready for it this morning, not yet.

"You know the kids are coming home for holidays tomorrow,

so, after I finish at the consulate, we're going directly to the bush-market. You can also stock up on provisions for the month. Are you listening to me?"

"Yes, my sister. Thank you, my sister. You alone know how to help a brother in trouble save some devalued CFA."

"Yes, a brother who wants to do a stupid thing like move to Santa Barbara, a new quartier of worthless, thieving, conniving snobs and politicians . . ."

"My sister, you're being silly. Haven't you heard that's where the power and the money now lie in this country?"

"Really? Where was it before, my brother? . . . I take it you'll be content with smelling the smoke from their kitchens and cigars, or watch starry-eyed as their Mercedeses and BMWs zoom by your little shack!"

On that note they both had a hearty laugh, the first real one since they shared their morning greetings. The ride to the consulate went smoothly, if smoothness still had any meaning in this city. Manda went through the demeaning procedure of putting her name on an appointment sheet that was dated two weeks from that day. The other days were already full, she was told. And all this for a transit visa. Of all the embassies and consulates in her city, this was the only one where one could wait for two weeks, or more, to obtain the right to apply for a visa. It was more than humiliating. It was a system of control that was as disgraceful, brutal, and unwarranted, like the rape that one of the female employees of this same consulate had suffered from a group of disgruntled young men who had ambushed her in town. They could not reach her boss, nor the institution he represented in their country, but she had been an easy target, a welcome outlet for lashing out at dehumanizing immigration politics. Manda had once missed a conference and had sworn never to forgive the people. It was extremely difficult to get sponsorship to international conferences. She had worked so hard for that one but the nonendorsable, nonrefundable ticket she had received three days before her departure date had required that she spend the day and night in Europe before connecting the next day. She had bluntly been told she had to take a rendezvous and return in ten days! So what if her conference was beginning in four days?

"Dommage, madame. Dommage. Those are the rules."

"I understand rules, but do the same rules apply for a transit visa?"

"Yes, of course."

"Even for a transit visa?"

"Suivant? Next!"

"And some bastards say we're basking in the sun of the postcolonial era!" she spat, straight into the other woman's face.

Manda does not know to this day how she made it home that day without killing someone. She had promised herself never to forgive, but in this country, she had mused, What would one forgive, and what wouldn't one forgive? This time, she was prepared not to miss her conference, come rain, come sun. She was expecting her ticket in two weeks and had decided to go put her name on the dreaded rendezvous list. Well, if she did not receive the ticket as promised, she would just have to keep bouncing her name from one list to another. "Hey! one has to survive, come rain, come sun, ooo!"

"What did you say?" Manoji asked his cousin.

"No, I was just thinking aloud."

"About what?"

"The market," she lied.

It happened two and half hours later, as they were returning from the market. Manda was driving towards the last turn, about four hundred metres from Manoji's apartment. She had considerably slowed down at the corner even though she had the right to drive on. In these days of devaluation and zero salary, one could not be too cautious. Most drivers willingly gave up their right-of-way to crazy drivers just to save their cars from being bumped. As she was negotiating the left turn, she suddenly caught sight of a yellow taxi coming forcefully from her left as well. She had to act immediately. It had to be her headlights or the driver's door. She ground on her brakes and braced herself. The taxi driver's right headlight slammed into her left headlight. Fortunately for Manda and the woman sitting in the passenger seat of the taxi, the violent contact drove both cars apart so that they remained locked in at the headlights, like bulls in a fight, but were sufficiently forced apart to form an inverted V. The taxi that had been following closely behind her was also caught in the jam. The driver had tried to elude the accident by swiftly swerving to Manda's right but the force of the impact with the other taxi drove the right rear end of her car into his left rear end. The three cars were locked in an N formation. Tyres could be heard screeching all around. Then the shouting and the screaming broke loose like hailstones on a zinc roof that salute the coming of the rains after a harsh dry season. The driver who had caused the accident was the first to jump out of his car.

"Je dis ee, la femme-ci, tu allais même où comme ça," he shouted, wagging his finger in her direction.

"Regardez-moi ça, vous les femmes, on vous donne le permis et vous ne savez même pas conduire . . ."

"Oui, ça doit être les permis-là qu'on achete . . ." a passenger in one of the taxis quipped.

"Heh! What did you say, you, what the hell did you say?" Manoji exploded, forcing his way out of the car and moving dangerously towards the taxi driver.

"Ah-hah, ah no be tok," he said with contempt, and the whole area exploded in laughter. "Ce sont les anglos. Ah say, eh ma broda, you no fit teach you sista how for drob moto, eeh? Na so weh dem di drob moto for wena condri, ee masa?"

"Oui, ça c'est la conduite de Bamenda," another passenger chimed, a wicked grin on his face.

Manoji felt as if he had been stung by a bee. He felt the bile flow into his bowels from all directions. All these people were having a good time at his and his sister's expense simply because he had opened his mouth and let a few English words escape.

"You fool, you damn fool," Manoji swore under his breath.

"Quoi, qu'est-ce que l'anglo-là dit?" the taxi driver asked, laughing furiously, his entire torso quavering, wiping away the tears from his eyes.

Before anyone could notice, Manoji took three swift steps and gave the driver a resounding blow. The injured man tried to return the blow, but another man swiftly placed his body between the two men, asking them not to begin a brawl. They had to hold the taxi driver's hands, although they could not seal his lips.

"Anglo!" he spat.

"You stupid, silly, uncouth, uneducated Frog. How dare you!"

Manda heard her cousin screaming.

"Please Manoji . . . my brother, please . . ."

"Regardez-moi ça. Regardez-moi les anglos-ci. Tu penses que tu es à Bamenda ici. Ils pensent toujours qu'ils sont plus intelligents que tout le monde. Ecoutez-le parler le ingrish ici. Ma frend, ah don speak ingrish. You speak ingrish?" The speaker let the laughter subside, but before Manoji could counter, he continued, "Regarde-moi un imbecile . . ."

"You call me an imbecile? You idiot!"

"Oui, imbecile, tu es idiot. Regarde-moi ça. Il fallait qu'on vous laisse avec le Nigeria, ces anglos. On a eu pitié de vous, on vous a accepté dans notre pays et au lieu de rester tranquille, vous venez nous casser les pieds pour rien."

"Your loose understanding of the history of this country is

so pathetic and farfetched that . . . What am I saying? It's because of fools like you that this country is where it is . . ."

"Tu entends? Il dit qu'il a pitié de toi. Villageois, est-ce que tu comprends le mot *patetik*?"

"Quoi? Anglos!" the man Manoji had interrupted sneered. "Il fallait qu'on vous laisse, tous ces, 'how dar you speek to me,' là-bas. Tout le monde chez vous est docta, tous le monde chez vous est ph.d., si on vous abandonnait avec le Nigeria, vous serrez tous civiliser par les Babangidas et les Abachas."

"Didons, ne prononce pas le nom d'un certain Abacha ici. L'anglofool-là qui veut nous prendre notre Bakassi. Les voleurs Nigerians . . ."

"Heh, dis-donc, le problème ici n'a rien a voir avec Abacha ou Bakassi. C'est vrai que les anglos sont tous parreils, des tordus, mais revenons à ce qui nous concerne ici. Vous les camerounais, vous êtes toujours comme ça. Tous, des fainéants. Tous, des fuireurs des problèmes."

Manda was still sitting in her car as if glued to her seat. She was following what was going on around her like a bad dream, a nightmare from which she would wake up and it would be over. Like so many things in this country, she marveled at the turn the altercation had taken. The insults flew back and forth about anglophones and francophones; then shifted to insults about the Bamis, the Betis, the Ewondos, the Bassas, Magidas, Bakwerians, Bamenda people. Tempers reached the final breaking point when party politics took centre stage. Loyalties broke ranks. They argued about parties like they would a football game: SDF against CPDM, CPDM against UPC, UPC against SDF, UPC against UNDP, and the matches were played and replayed, the balls rolling dangerously from one side of the field to the other.

Manda watched the crowd and the whole scene suddenly became comical to her. The frustrations buried in the hearts of her people were being tragically displayed either through their ignorance, their strong biases, or even hatred. Their arguments betrayed linguistic, cultural, and political assumptions whose validity they no longer particularly cherished, nor cared about. They had reached a point in their historical and political evolution where it sufficed to hear a word of English or French, detect a particular accent, and racial slurs and stereotypes would flow in abundance like palmwine at a death celebration. What had happened to national unity? This scene had become all too familiar in a city and country where people were disenchanted with almost everything around them; where political, linguistic, and tribal affinities had become the fertile ground for the rehashing of old wounds and the settling of old scores, no matter how minute. The crowd had all but forgotten the accident that had brought them together in the first place. The accident had become a sideshow. And after what seemed like an eternity to Manda, the police squad finally arrived, drew up the accident sketch, and the three drivers appended their signatures.

Six months passed. Then Manda received a summons letter to appear in court. She was whistling and smiling all the way. She had nothing to worry about. It would be over in a few minutes. But the accident sketch placed in front of her looked nothing like what she had signed a few months earlier. She stared blankly at the piece of paper.

"Do you recognise this sketch, madam?"

"No, I do not."

"What do you mean you do not?"

"Really, I don't. This doesn't look anything like the sketch of the accident I was involved in."

"Madam, did you not have an accident on such and such a day, at such and such a time, at such and such a place?"

"Yes, I did."

"So, what is this go-for-before-for-back? Eh? This is the

sketch of that accident. It has been in your file since the day of the accident."

"I tell you this is not that sketch."

"Are you trying to accuse us of wrongdoing, madam?"

"No, that's not what I said."

"Then what are you saying, MADAM?"

"All I am saying is . . ."

"Madam, please don't waste our time. We have a lot work to do here. Maybe you don't, but we do . . . Is this your signature? Yes or no?"

"Yes, it is," she replied, noticing the signature for the first time.

"Are you sure this is your signature?"

Manda just stared, nodding her head, and unexpectedly broke into uncontrollable peals of laughter that shook her entire body and soul.

8

Bayam-Sellam

"Aagh, will you stop pulling my scalp like that . . . ?"

"But Mother, you should sit still. I can't braid this hair if you keep jumping around like a rabid dog . . ."

"Hmm, wunna see me baluck. Dis pikin want kill me or na weti . . . aaaghh . . . Pikin go drag me biebieh soteh kanda for my head di come commot, ghmm, badluck."

"Mami, na weti now . . . a beg shiddon quiet . . . so so shake your head, so so shake shake your head . . . how man go fit plat hair so?"

"Ah swear to God, dis pikin want kill me . . . for sharp morning time so . . ."

Grace swore under her breath, put both hands on her mother's shoulders, and pushed her firmly down on the stool. But the mother would not sit still. She was agitated, moving her buttocks on the stool as if she were sitting on an army of red ants. She was pivoting from right to left, moving her head up and down, all the while talking, to no one in particular. She talked and cursed, cursed and talked. The mother was restless. Grace did not like working with the mother when she was in one such moods. She had already braided four rows of hair. It was now too late to defect from the task. The thought of leaving the mother walking around with hair sticking up on half of her skull was amusing. Mother is crazy enough to do that, she thought. Not that the mother's eccentricities bothered her. But she cared about the insults and the mother's mouth running nonstop about what a bad daughter she had, who would leave her mother walking around with a head like a porcupine's back. The mother was capable of this and much more. Grace did not need the aggravation. She tried to ignore the mother. It was definitely going to be one of those mornings. The mother was raving and cursing at everyone, angry at herself, at the world, and at no one in particular. Grace placed her hands on the mother's head and ran her thumbs down the lines of the rows of hair she was braiding. They were straight and shiny. She brushed the hair flat beside the new row she was about to begin braiding. The hair stuck up in the air towards her face. She gathered some hair between her fingers and proceeded to weave it as fast as she could, quietly hoping the mother would sit still.

She longed for one of those quiet, uneventful days when her mother would fall asleep on the stool as her fingers scraped and stroked her mother's warm scalp while her thighs struggled to hold her mother's shoulders and head in place. Grace wished her mother were sitting still on the stool; she, on the ground, her body between her mother's thighs, her legs spread out in front of her as her mother picked strand of hair after strand of hair, weaving them expertly while the smells of ingredients, food, and work drifted from her mother's body and lulled her to sleep.

Suddenly, the mother moved her head so fast the hair slipped through her fingers. Again. Grace tried to hold onto the hair she was holding between her right thumb and middle finger. The mother screamed and jumped off the stool. The mother rushed into the house and was out in no time, her fa-mous faded blue exercise book in her hands. Grace looked up at the sky, rolled her eyes, sighed, asked God what she had done to deserve this, and then sat down, her arms falling by her sides. She picked up the comb that had come flying out of the mother's hair, shut the mother's voice out, and started playing with the teeth of the comb.

Mi Ngiembuh, a.k.a. Mami Christopher, or Ma Christo for short, looked nothing like the stereotypical bayam-sellam one meets everyday in the markets: tall, huge, large biceps, ten-pound breasts held defiantly in check by worn-out okrika breastwears with secret pockets sewn in for keeping wads of money. No, Mi Ngiembuh was small in stature, about one metre fifty two, lean, and mean, or so her rivals charged. It was the smallness of her body and the childlike look on her thin face that misled people into dismissing her. But they soon learned not to underestimate her, for under that innocent de-meanor, that easily infatuating smile, beat the heart of a tiger—her family totem—and the rage of a hungry lioness. She had paid her dues and risen to the top of the food retail business. When people grumbled about how much of the food market she now controlled, they easily forgot her humble be-ginnings. She got married when she was seventeen to a car-penter who was quite happy making furniture for people's homes, and sometimes building their houses too. The man's mind was always bustling with new ideas and his fingers worked wonders with bamboo, cane, and wood. His wife often boasted that her husband's gift was bestowed by the gods to one person per generation, for the man could do such strange things with his raw material that one had difficulty recognis-ing bamboo or cane or wood for what they really were when he produced a masterpiece. She would often sit at a distance, a look of curiosity and contentment on her face, and watch as his fingers stroked the wood or cane so intimately it was sometimes embarrassing. There was no doubt in her mind: the gods had blessed her husband's hands. But some years into her marriage, Mi Ngiembuh got increasingly bored with the smells of wood and bamboo littering her parlour, her veranda, her yard. Her sense of smell was slowly but quietly falling asleep. There had been a time when lying on her bed, with her eyes closed, she could suck the air wafting through the door into her lungs and tell exactly what piece of furniture her husband was working on. But time passed and she began to notice the wood and bamboo only when her toes hit against them. If her husband was hurt by this gradual loss of interest, he said nothing about it. He blamed her inattention on the wifely and motherly duties that had taken over his wife's life. But Mi Ngiembuh wasn't one to dissuade him from such a conclusion. On the contrary, she borrowed a small amount of money from her spouse, began what she called a small business, and diverted her energies elsewhere. And she did start small. She would leave Bamenda, go to Bali market on its big-market days and buy three or four bags of garri, take them back with her to Bamenda, and retail the garri, right there in front of her house, to her neighbours. At first, she only had a stool on which she placed a huge basin in which she would pour the garri and use a tin cup to measure and sell it. Soon enough, she got bored with selling this lone item. As the seasons came and went, her enterprising flair changed with them. She quickly became like water, taking the form of any vessel that was at her disposal. Her husband worked magic with wood, she worked magic with food. She branched into buying and selling cocoyams, fresh and dried groundnuts, yams, sweet potatoes, corn, okra, plantains. The sole, lonely garri-stool was soon displaced by an extension, a room she built right in front of the house, one that now gave her house an **L** shape. She designed the room in such a way that a large window was built into the wall that faced the street. When opened, the large flap of wood reclined towards the street and would serve as a table on which samples of the wares she had inside the room could be displayed. The seller could then sit in the room all day and carry out transactions with customers through the open window. But again, Mi Ngiembuh wasn't one to limit her retail business to her home. She soon started courting the market women who bought food in bulk from wholesalers and retailed it at their own pace in the main market. This had been her biggest challenge. In the cutthroat business world of bayam-sellam, enemies could easily be made and people could easily get hurt. Mi Ngiembuh knew she had to devise her own way of dealing with the small-business, day-to-day market women. Walking up to them in open market and trying to convince them had not worked. Many treated her with suspicion, many didn't want to give up the alliances they had forged with other bayam-sellams for many years. So, she changed tactics. She identified the most influential of the market women and paid them visits at home. She was nonthreatening and cajoled them with promises of lower prices and a better future for women and their children. Women can run the world if they stick together, if they listen to each other, she enthused. Her infatuating smile and guileless words charmed them. One by one, the market women bought from her first before buying from other bayam-sellams. This woman of small stature, this woman who was often underestimated by potential rivals until she unleashed her fangs, this small woman, known to the market women only as Mami Christo and affectionately called Big-Sister, had slowly but quietly built an empire. She had her pulse on the seasons, on the surrounding farming communities, and on the loyal group of market women who had also become part of her family, part of her life. She demanded and nurtured their loyalty the same way she had kept the driver of her battered four-wheel-drive Toyota pickup truck for years until a terrible accident claimed his life. It happened during the rainy season, when the roads were at their most treacherous. Fonki, the driver, off-loaded his boss and passengers at the bottom of the hill, jumped into the driver's seat, made a joke about eating this hill alive, and gunned the engine. The passengers held their breath and watched as the engine accelerated in short, fast bursts and the truck danced dangerously from one side of the hill to the other, cutting sharp corners briskly as it zigzagged up, up, up. He was almost at the top of the hill when the comforting sound of acceleration was snuffed from the engine. Silence fell everywhere. Even the birds and insects seemed to have heard the engine die. To the passengers horror, the truck began to career down the slope. Fonki clutched and clutched, trying to reignite the engine, all the while braking furiously and managing to control the truck from driving off the hill. When the engine wouldn't start, he opened the driver's door, stuck his head out in order to see the slope and better control the tyres as they cascaded down the slippery, muddy, treacherous road. Suddenly, he hit the embankment to his right and the truck veered to his left so violently that it tipped over, the two tyres on the right side hanging in the air and spinning aimlessly. Fearing the worst, Fonki tried to jump out of the vehicle, but in his desperate attempt to save himself, his chest got caught between the open door and the frame as the truck came bearing down on him. The weight of the bags of cocoyams that had given the truck stability as it struggled up the hill were now bearing the vehicle down, sucking the life out of him. The screaming, horrified passengers ran up the hill as fast as they could. They put their heads and hands together and struggled to lift up the truck and free their driver. They freed his ribs from the torture but they couldn't save his life. With no other car in sight to take his battered body to a hospital they watched silently as he died in Mi Ngiembuh's arms. This was one among many of the realities she had learned to live with in this business. But the challenge she was facing this morning as her daughter desperately tried to finish braiding her hair was different from the many crises she had fought and survived in the past. She had had a sleepless night and the restlessness had transported her spirit through dawn and spilled over into the new day. One look at the way the wrappa was tied firmly around the buttocks, over her kaba ngondo, sucking in the folds of the gown, said it all. Mi Ngiembuh was restless. She was holding the faded blue exercise book in her hand, skimming through the pages, and pacing up and down. Her husband often joked that this blue book was one of her children, her oldest and dearest child. He joked that this book was as old, tough, and mean as its owner. The faded blue exercise book was her business bible. It was her life. It contained all the names of her debtors and how much they cumulatively owed her over the years. Everything was well charted: names, orders, places, amounts paid, amounts owed . . . If there was one thing her children had learned over the years, it was *never* to touch her blue book, except when they were sent for it. This book held the key to her success with her market women. She was known to be tough as nails, but the women also loved her because she gave them a long rope to pull when it came to paying their debts. When Mi Ngiembuh felt that a customer was taking undue liberties with her generosity, she simply drove her truck to the market and, in broad daylight, confiscated all her goods. The women dreaded the shame of such public exposure more than the confiscation of their goods, so no matter how much they owed, they made sure they paid their debt, no mater how small the installments. The system had worked and then they woke one day and were greeted by a strange friend calling himself economic crisis. They watched the stranger with suspicion for his arrival had forced them to rearrange their lives at every turn, in order to accommodate his demands. But he became a greedy monster who soon controlled their markets and took over their lives. They waited for him to leave but days, months, years went by and the stranger seemed to be getting more and more comfortable, sleeping in the bed that had been offered him. He had outstayed his welcome but refused adamantly to admit it or leave. Buyers who visited the women in their markets began to pay lower prices for their goods and the answers to their pleas always were, "c'est la crise" or "mami, na crise ya, man go do how no?" The more the women protested, the more they were told to protest to the government, after all, no be na wunna government bring this ting say crise économique? Me ah know say crise économique na weti? Wunna go ask wunna gobna. Crise, crise, crise, . . . everywhere they looked, crise économique was laying eggs; everywhere they looked crise économique was incubating; everywhere they turned, crise économique's eggs were hatching locusts. Some of the women were forced to abandon the food retail business and seek other ways of making a living. It was only a matter of time, they were saying. Even then, the women never imagined that this unwelcome visitor was only the beginning of more and worse to come. They went to sleep yet another night and woke up to find that their visitor had invited another fat-cow friend of his. This one was greedier, his appetite insatiable. He had a sweet-sounding name—SAP—but this sap was nothing like the sap the men tapped from raffia or palm trees. SAP sucked them dry like a leech and grew fatter with their blood each waking day. As the days went by, he needed more and more of their blood, and so, he ordered massive layoffs, which the people quickly nicknamed compression. He cut civil servants' salaries by sixty percent, and to add insult to injury, ordered the devaluation of the CFA franc. This final act was like a death warrant issued to the market women. Inflation skyrocketed. Glass-eyed buyers ambled through their stalls, dragging their feet as if weighed down by bags of cement, parroting words and phrases the women didn't want to hear: c'est la crise maman; na crise économique; na compression; deh dong compresser me . . . Some women closed down their stalls because they could no longer pay the rent. Women whose husbands had been compressé had to seek alternate ways of taking care of their families and sometimes this meant pulling their daughters out of school to share in their increased responsibilities, within and outside the home; sometimes it meant resorting to prostitution.

Mi Ngiembuh watched with consternation as the empire she had built with her sweat and blood began slowly to crumble. Her customers debts were piling up. She was now keeping count in a ledger. Worst of all, this wahala was depleting her resources. That was the point of no return for her. She told her daughter she wasn't going to sit down and let crise économique and his allies take away the business that had taken her a lifetime to build. She opened the exercise book in her hand, flipped through the old, worn-out sheets, and took in a deep breath. You might have lost the shine of your skin, she was saying to the yellowish-brown sheets, but I'll be damned before someone forces me to lose mine.

"Masafi, go into the house and get your wrappa. Bring my headtie. We have work to do . . ."

"What kind of work?" her daughter asked, dashing into the house, excitement building in her bones.

"We're going to the market to call on all my women. Where's your father?"

Papa Christo stuck his head through the door. He wondered what the commotion was all about. One never knew with his strong-headed, mouth-running wife.

"Papa Christo, will you drive me to the market, please?"

Pa Christo was not fooled. He knew it was an order. One look at her half-braided hair and the veins sticking through her forearms as she strangled her waist with the wrappa said it all. Her face might look calm and collected but he knew her insides were churning like the pool collecting the spill at the end of a waterfall. He thought she looked insane with that head of unfinished hair and those deep, expressionless eyes. He also knew one thing, something terrible was about to happen. He took the keys of the truck from his wife hands and walked to the vehicle. His wife and daughter hopped in beside him.

The meeting started at exactly seven o'clock. The women had all congregated at Mi Ngiembuh's house, every single one of them. The market closed its gates at six o'clock and she had given them one hour to be at her house. When the last women walked in, she shut and locked the door, barricading them inside.

"I have called this meeting because of the situation we are all going through. First, they said the economic crisis we were dealing with would be taken care of and everything was going to go back to normal. We believed them. And then the days went by. Then months went by. Then years went by and nothing happened . . ."

"No, something happened . . ."

"Structural Adjustment Programmes . . ."

"Yes, and we all know how much these programmes have saved us . . ."

"As if that weren't enough, they took away—and with impunity, I might add—the little money that civil servants make in this country . . . How do you go to sleep one night, wake up in the morning, and hear that your salary has been slashed by eighty, or is it sixty, percent?"

"And then French people look at us, they laugh at us, and they say, you know what, we're tired of spoon-feeding you. (That's what those leeches say.) We're tired of carrying you on our backs, they say. We have to wean you right now. (How can they wean us when they're the ones who have been sucking

our breasts dry?) Here, we are devaluing your CFA by fifty
percent . . . patati patata."

"Yes, the devaluation has hurt us, but what has our own
government done to help us?" Mami Mary, the big sister of all
the market women asked, pointedly.

"I'll tell you," she continued. "Our government has not
done one damned thing for us. Look at how other west and
central African countries have dealt with the situation. Mami
Agha, you're the one who goes to Libreville, Cotonou, Abidjan
to buy bazin. What have they done for their people in those
countries?"

"They've increased the salaries of civil servants instead . . ."

"Doesn't that make sense, eh, my sisters? Devaluation . . .
salary increase. Yet the workers here were handed another
salary reduction after devaluation and what did they do? . . .
Nothing."

"This is a country of cowards, I tell you. All these men, no
marrow in their bones. The government says salary cut and
what do they do? They go to bars, soak themselves in barrels
of beer, afofo, odontol, kembe fédéral, haa, arki, you name it,
and go to sleep. The government says devaluation and they
throw up their hands. The government says salary cut and
they stick their tails between their legs and walk around like
frightened animals. And now, everywhere you turn, people are
singing one song, "compression." Sometimes I'm so enraged I
feel like compressé-ing their heads right through their bodies.
Just flatten the thing down to a pulp. God, how many more
people will lose their jobs before something is done?"

"Hear her, hear her. We're holding your feet, our sister . . ."

"And while this is going on, we, the women, are carrying
the cross. Not just our own but everyone else's. We're bearing
the brunt of . . ."

"Exactly. Mami Mary, that's precisely why I asked all of you
to come here tonight. We have to do something . . . We, the

women and mothers, are the ones suffering the most from the current situation. We're the ones selling the food in the market that people now want for free. We're the ones who have to go home in the evening and make excuses to our children about not being able to buy their books, their uniforms, not to talk of paying their fees. We're the ones who have to face the shame of taking our children out of school. We're the ones who now sit and watch helplessly as our children die from simple diseases like diarrhoea, cough, and fever, because we can no longer afford the medicines. We, and our daughters, are the ones putting our bodies on the meat market for slaughter and consumption. I am saying that we're the life blood of this community and we have to force the community to do something about it . . ."

"Mami Christo, what do you have in mind?" Mami Agha asked guardedly.

A cloud fell over Big Sister's face. Her cheek bones stood firm, like granite. This was the mask the women never liked to see.

"I want us to close the food market down."

Big Sister's words drew a loud gasp. Some of the women started talking excitedly to each other, some openly saying that Mami Christo had finally gone insane, but others sat in stoned silence. The surprise announcement had impounded their words.

"Mami Christo, why would you say a thing like that?" Mami Mary asked, standing up, undoing and retying her wrappa firmly around her waist. "The food market is all we market women have. How can you even suggest that we burn the bridge we're standing on, knowing full well that the crocodiles are patiently waiting?"

"My sisters, I'm not crazy. Hear me out. Have you asked yourself the question, Why, after all we've just discussed, people haven't revolted against the government? You cut salaries, you devalue the CFA, you cut salaries, inflation keeps going up, and people sit and grumble at home like children? Drunken men sit at home and pick fights with their wives. I've come to believe that the reason lies in the abundance of food in this country. So long as no one goes hungry, no one really cares to fight . . . How many times have we slashed our prices to liquidate our stock before it gets bad? . . . How many times?"

"You have a point there. People might walk naked, they might not pay their children's school fees, but so long as they go to bed each night on a full stomach . . ."

"Mami Mary, I hear what you're saying but what Big Sister is asking us to do is to shoot ourselves in the leg and then think we can stand up and walk to the farm," one of the women who had been listening silently to the discussion protested.

"Mami Anna, you're right. We have to be careful when we spit in the wind, for it might blow back into our faces. All I'm saying is, let's go on strike. Let's shut down the food market for . . ."

"Yes, why don't you just ask us to kill ourselves, you money-woman?" Mami Joe asked, disdain in her voice. "It's easy for you to stand here and say what you're saying, after all you have your money, we're just poor women waiting for you to throw your crumbs at us."

This challenge was greeted by another loud gasp. The women knew that Mami Joe and Mami Christopher hated each other. They both tolerated the presence of the other out of respect for and harmony of the group. Mami Joe often gossiped about Mami Christo behind her back. She accused her of belonging to a nyongo secret society that used human sacrifice to build its wealth. She often pointed out that Fonki's death had not been an accident. Mami Christo sold that boy in nyongo to go and make more money for her boss in the other world, Mami Joe intimated. Some of the women fired back that Fonki wasn't the first driver to die on those roads, others accused Mami Joe of being jealous of Big Sister, but there were also those who believed Mami Joe. They remained in awe of Mami Christo and refused to break their alliance with her for fear of being sucked into her world of witchcraft and nyongo.

"Mami Joe, you're the one shooting yourself in the foot right now," Mami Agha interjected. "Of all of us sitting here, you owe this money-woman more money than the debts of ten women put together. You're like the bird that forgets, but remember, the trap doesn't . . ."

"Uhhh-huhh," the women chorused.

"What we're talking about here is very serious indeed . . . at least for those of us who consider ourselves women, mothers, and daughters. Mami Christo is right, we're the matches that will light the gunpowder that has been lying cold like ash. If we don't take this step, who will . . . ?"

"Yes, stand there and support your witch-friend," Mami Joe retorted, still stung by Mami Agha's rebuke.

The victim never saw it coming. Mami Agha was a huge woman but she could move her body faster than most women sitting in the crowded room. She took two quick steps and slammed Mami Joe's head against the wall.

Wulililililililili . . . the room exploded in confusion. Na which kana baluck dis now? the women were asking each other as Mami Joe struggled to her feet, spewing insults at Mi Ngiembuh and Mami Agha.

"Hum, ah no be talk! Ah be know say women dem no fit shiddon so talk sonting like correck people wey fight no commot. Which kana badluck dis now? Woman palava na so-so so," one of the women said scornfully, throwing her hands in the air.

"Mami Joe must commot for dis house, if no be so, dis meeting no go finish. We no fit continue dis meeting if dat witch woman still dey inside dis house," Mami Agha thundered.

She was untying and retying her wrappa so fast that the women had to make a decision. Mami Joe was booted out of the meeting. It took them a few more minutes to calm down and for the meeting to proceed.

"My sisters, I worry about one thing," Mami Mary said cautiously.

"What's that?" the others chorused.

"If we shut down the food market, we will be hurting ourselves and our families. Secondly, I wonder whether this will make a difference. Problems have made people become so blasé in this country that I wonder how effective our strike will be, if at all."

There was silence in the room. Mami Christo finally spoke after what seemed like an entire night had flirted by.

"My sisters, what I'm asking us to do is a very difficult thing indeed. But we're daughters of women who have spent their lives fighting and have taught us how to fight and fend for ourselves. Our mothers have left us many examples to guide us. I'll mention one. When there was that land dispute between cattle grazers and farmers, some seventy kilometres away from us here, who helped resolved that problem?"

"Women," the women chorused.

"What did you say?" Mami Christo asked, pulling the lobe of her right ear with her fingers.

"We said, women did it," the women chorused again.

"Yes, those women strapped their children on their backs and trekked those seventy kilometres, paying no heed to the sun that burnt through their skins, the sun that pounded the foreheads of their children. Those women braved the rains that poured down on them as if the heavens were mourning the loss of their queen. No, they trekked those seventy kilometres, got here, and camped out in front of the governor's house. And what did he do? This very man who for five years had been promising to resolve the land dispute, but sat here in his big office on the hill and instead took bribes from both sides, what did that pig do? He had to hire a tipper-truck to carry the women back. He had to go back with them to see for himself, and what do you know, the land dispute was resolved. Why . . . ?"

"Because the women took action."

"Yes, because women took action. We've watched as things have gone downhill. We're the ones who cradle our children in our arms and our tears cannot explain why they can't go to school, why they can't have books, why we can't pay the fees . . . it's our tears that explain the things we can't. It's our tears that our children no longer understand . . ."

"Yes, we have to do this," one of the women added, jumping up from her seat. "It's the food grown by the farmers of our area that supplies most of the big cities. Those big bayam-sellams from the big cities depend on us. They depend on our farms. They depend on our labour. If we shut down the food market, then the big cities will suffer. Imagine that. Imagine what that means to city folk, to the country . . ."

"We don't know where this is going to take us, but we know it will strike a chord somewhere . . ."

"And might even earn us another state of emergency . . ."

The women had laughed as their meeting came to a close, but they had not realised their sister's words might indeed have been prophetic. Two weeks into the strike of the market women, the powers-that-be declared a state of emergency for their region. The women smiled when they heard the news. They were used to fighting enemies more formidable than army tanks and tear gas. This wasn't the first state of emergency slapped on them and their families. They knew it wasn't going to be the last.

9

Slow Poison

Manoji was lying on the bamboo bed his mother had placed in the parlour, positioned in a strategic corner where he could see the sunlight, if and when he was able to turn his head to face the nsaa. Yes, the nsaa, the sun; the two who now watched obsessively over him ever since the people stopped coming, ever since the relatives fled. Manoji painstakingly turned his head, each movement an effort that could kill him. His neck was rigid, the bones in his back creaked, his arms refused to follow directions meted out by an equally numb mind. The bones in his feet seemed to crackle, his knees knocked against each other, and he let out a quiet moan. He thought it might take him an entire day to turn his head, at least he hoped it was daylight. He had long lost the ability to stay in focus, to synchronise his being with trivial things like day or night. But he had to see the sun, that much he was certain of. He wanted to stare at the golden streaks slashing through the foliage of huge trees, burning through the eyelids of children who mocked its power, defied its scorching manhood, and played to the tunes of juvenile dreams. He wanted to feel those dreams again and again . . . He wanted to see the sun, no, he wanted to feel the rays burn through his brown (or was it rosy-pink?) parched skin. He wanted to feel the sun on his estranged epidermis, toasting his emaciated, lifeless body and to taste the stench of burning fat in his mouth, in his nostrils, in his belly. He turned. One more inch, he told himself. He knew that inch would cost him. He shut his eyes, and just as he was about to make the move, called one memory to his rescue. Each memory lent him the support he needed to move his head an inch. Rememorying took over, fighting the aches in his head, in his neck, in his body, with the fierceness of a hen protecting her young ones from the penetrating gaze of a very patient but hungry hawk. Rememorying numbed the pain and, inch by inch, Manoji's face came into full view of the sun.

He gazes at the sun, his eyes wide open, blinking with the curiosity of a newborn discovering and pondering the world of humans. He suddenly feels an urge to stand, to lift his body, to stand up and walk; no, to float towards the sun. The hunger of a curious child who will not be daunted by vain threats is burning in him, through him. He has to stand up. He has to. He speaks to his legs. "Have I ever eaten and not shared with you?" he asks them. "Never," they reply. He doesn't know why, but his legs actually move. He is pulling his knees up and they are saying, yes, go ahead, let's hit the floor, let's stand. He is dreaming, yes, but a good dream. He can feel his body swinging precariously upright. He is nauseated and has to place his bony hands on his knees to steel himself. Every effort, every single effort costs him. A lot. But he refuses to be paralysed by the fear that threatens to glue his body to his bed. He has to fight the invisible paws that are forcing him to the ground. He lifts his hands from his knees and places them on the bamboo bed. He can feel the softness of the foam mattress his mother bought for him, the one she spent her savings on to give his bones some temporary relief. Most times, he couldn't notice the mattress was there. But sometimes he was grateful for her sacrifice. He moves his fingers and clutches its softness. His fingers say they are alive. He thinks he is alive. He awakens to being alive and smiles, in spite of himself. The mattress smells so much of death, how could he be alive?

He raises his head, holds firmly onto the exposed bamboo and concentrates on the brightness advancing through the open door, almost sucking him into its vortex. He grinds his teeth, lifts his torso and he is in the air. He can feel his feet on the floor. The house is quiet and he can hear the silence buzzing through his head. He begins to feel dizzy but knows he cannot afford to give in to the spasm moving like a wave through his bowels. And so he fixes his gaze on the receding shadow of the door and stares. He concentrates on the rays of the sun and stares. He moves towards them, gliding through space. He feels he is falling. He thinks he is falling and desperately grabs at anything he can touch. His hands can feel the firmness of wood. He clings to it, braces himself, and opens his eyes. He recognises the door frame. He runs his fingers, a few inches, up and down the mahogany as if scratching a lover's back. He desires its firmness. He longs for its ageless demeanor of defiance. He is about to take a step forward when something catches his eyes. The image is bleary. He has to still himself and focus. An image is reflected back at him. It seems to be projected from within the far reaches of the closet, of the mirror hanging on the brick wall. He stills himself and waits. The image is moving closer, zooming in. He is struck dumb, startled by the old man staring back blankly at him. The face looks curiously familiar. It displays marks and features peculiar to his family. The prominent forehead, like his uncle's; the prominent, high cheek bones, like his mother's; the full head of kinky hair, the protruding, stubborn chin, like his father's. But the eyes, the haunting, scared eyes of a caged animal, whose eyes are these? Eyes like those of an owl. Eyes that look too big for his face; eyes that seem to be popping out of their sockets; eyes whose whiteness is frightening, a whiteness that seems to spread, overpowering the blackness of the face, highlighting two deep, dark pupils, spinning like a whirlpool at the bottom of a well. Manoji cannot place these eyes. He cannot place this bony face. He makes a supreme effort to lift his hands and feel the bones sticking through the cheeks. What is left of them. But the hands divert his attention from the face. The thin, long fingers, with their overgrown nails look like claws. They are skeletal and remind him of the hands of the scarecrows he used to make with his father when he was a young boy and proudly display in his mother's farms. He tries to imitate the movement of the scarecrow's hands, agitating, stirring excitedly with the force of the wind, but the hands remain hanging in mid-air. They are refusing to follow his command. He cannot bear to look at those fingers. His hands slowly drop by his side. He can hear his clavicles creak. His gaze follows the clavicles down his bare torso. Manoji stares at his scrawny, wasted body. The brownness of his skin seems to have been bleached away, leaving behind an almost transparent pinkish surface. The dermis is disrobed, ugly in its nakedness. He traces the long lines carefully designed and left bare by exposed ribs. They are nothing like the tiger's, nothing like the zebra's. He can see the thin layer of flesh clinging desperately to the bones as he struggles to breathe in and out. Caught between the hollow lines are spots, huge dark spots. They are nothing like the leopard's. Some of the spots look like scars that leave an imprint on the skin after a bout of yaws. They are competing with shingles and scabies for space. He is thankful for the hard, dark crusts of the shingles that taunt him with a semblance of blackness. He knows these spots are bearing witness to the poison that has slowly but tenaciously been devouring his body, eating away his life. He has become a bag of bones. He has become a scarecrow. He fidgets with the wrappa wrapped around his waist. What is left of it. The wrappa falls to the ground. He doesn't hear a sound. He looks with bitterness at the two straight sticks that used to be thighs; he wants to knock on the protruding, round knees. He tries to make a fist but his fingers will not indulge him. He suddenly realises he has missed something. He can't tell what it is. He has to think. What am I forgetting? he is desperately asking himself. He needs a memory, right now. He needs a memory to ignite his brain again. He is feeling dizzy. He wants to throw up, but there is nothing to throw up. He clutches the firmness of the mahogany, stills himself and the old man in the mirror comes back in focus. The man is missing something, something between his bony thighs. Where is his manhood? What is this shriveled up, almost unnoticeable appendage, clinging ferociously to the pubis? Or what is left of it? It looks almost like a stamp, affixed on an envelope. Manoji is feeling dizzy; he is choking; he is coughing; he cannot hold his sides, he cannot hold onto the mahogany. Its firmness is letting him go. He feels his hands gliding off the wood. He is falling. Falling. Floating backwards to the ground. He feels as light as a wisp of smoke. He wants to see the sun. He wants to wrap his body in the folds of its golden warmth. He wants to remain suspended in its splendour. But he is falling. Falling. The last thing he glimpses in the mirror is the familiar face of his mother. She is standing, silently, right behind him. Their eyes meet. He can feel the heat. The sun is right there with him. He can feel its warmth enveloping his body, seeping through his bag of bones, melting the marrow, taking over his memories. He knows they will be kept in a safe place for him. He lets himself fall. Her arms are open. He is grateful he is falling into her waiting arms.

Manoji died the way he had lived: in the arms of a woman.

At least that was the one thing, the one ounce of consolation he grasped firmly in the palms of his bony hands, in the wiry folds of his shriveled-up heart, when his spirit quietly and calmly abandoned his body, or what was left of it. My son passed away in my arms. I was sitting on the floor, holding him firmly to my chest, oblivious to the silence, the loneliness, the abandon that was threatening to sweep me away. I sat there, the hard floor beneath me, the only thing that reminded me I was still alive. Even as I held my son's lifeless body, I adamantly refused to accept his death. He is still alive, I kept saying to myself. It's not possible. He can't be gone, I kept consoling myself. But then, his usual paper-light body began slowly and slowly to weigh down on me like a basin of water. I began to wonder how this had all happened. How had this lit-tle baby I carried just a few months ago on my back as I cleaned the house, as I cooked food, as I worked on the farm, as I went to the market, how had this baby come to this? When did this all begin? When? How had this happened to us? To our lives? I couldn't think straight. I knew I needed his memories. I needed to rememory his life in order to do the right thing for my son, in order to set him free. There was no time for tears. There was no place for tears. I held him firmly to my chest and his memories took over. I needed them to con-sume me the way they had consumed his body.

A few years ago, Manoji started going out with young women unusually bigger than the ones I had always seen him with. It isn't that he hadn't had big women friends before. This time was different. He stuck to big women only. I pointed this new preference out to him. "My son, why are you going out with all these fat women? What's wrong with you? Is this the new craze?" I asked him. Humm, Manoji smiled and re-minded me that the women were just "bigger." They are true African women, he enthused. True African women with flesh on their bones, he parroted. But I was not to be fooled and I kept on teasing him. One day, as he was about to walk away after one such conversation (I called them conversations, he called them unnecessary snooping on my part), he changed his mind and walked back into my house. He pulled up a chair, sat down by the fire, put those long hands calmly on his knees, and asked me an embarrassing question.

"Mother," he said.

"Yes, my son. What is it?"

"Have you heard about this thing they call AIDS?"

"What's that my son?"

"Come on mother, you know what it is. Stop pretending not to know."

"No, I don't know what it is. What is it?"

"Mother, you know it's an illness."

"An illness. What kind of illness?"

"Mother, you know what illness it is. You know it's that terrible disease people call 'slow poison.'"

"Slow poison? Are you talking to me about those lies those your people from the Ministry of Health are spreading around the country?"

"Mother, they're not lies. You heard what that doctor said the other day at the community meeting."

"I know what he was saying. He was talking about a disease that eats people away, slowly, as if they had taken slow poison. But my son, only people struck with witchcraft can suffer such a disease. This is not something the white people and those strangers from the Ministry of Health should come here and talk to us about. What do they know about our witchcraft? What do they know about esotericism? Nothing. Absolutely nothing. I tell you they know nothing about our abilities to manipulate the natural and the supernatural, how can they know about slow poison? . . ."

"But mother, this is serious . . ."

"Say what you want my son, but let me tell you something.

If those liars keep on coming here and talking about this so-called new disease that kills people slowly like the slow poison we cast on our enemies, then they will all suffer the same fate . . ."

"But mother, they say this slow poison is different from our own. It is different because you get it by having sexual relations with a man or a woman who already has the poison in them."

"So, why sleep with a woman who has been poisoned, my son?"

"You don't know she is."

"Impossible. How can you not know when a woman has been poisoned. If you can't, then you are not my son . . ."

"That's why my women are all plump . . . they have good blood, unlike thin women. You can't be sure of their blood . . ."

I knew what my son meant when he talked about bad blood. It had to do with our neighbour, a father who for three years had consistently given blood for his sickle-cell anemic child. But things never used to be like that. Over the years, his eight-year-old son had been given blood by almost every relative or friend living in this neighbourhood. Previously, when the child got ill, three, four, or five of us would go to the blood bank with the father and they would systematically collect our blood, test it, and then give the right blood to the child. And then things changed. They claimed the government had run out of money. That testing of blood from many people had become too expensive. They even started charging five thousand francs to cover the cost of each blood bag. If you have four people with you, that means twenty thousand. Imagine that. Who can afford that? People couldn't afford to give blood anymore. So now they pretest a sample and only collect the blood if the donor's blood is the right one. That's how our neighbour ended up as sole donor for his son. He gave his blood, gave his blood, gave his blood, and then one day the doctor said his blood was bad and could not be given to his son.

"How is that possible?" he asked the doctor.

"Your blood isn't good anymore," the doctor said.

"What do you mean, anymore? . . . I've been giving blood for three years and suddenly my blood isn't good? How? Has my blood group changed?"

"No, your blood group is still the same. But your blood now has a disease. Have you heard about AIDS? . . . Your blood is HIV-positive. That means your blood has a disease and I can't give your blood . . . I can't give the disease in your blood to your child . . ."

"I do not understand . . . I don't understand . . ."

"I understand . . ."

"No doctor, you don't understand. You know my son has sickle-cell anemia . . . He needs my blood or he'll die . . . Who's going to give my child blood? Who? . . . And now you're telling me I must stop. You're telling me I'm going to kill my child. You're telling me I'm going to die. You're sitting here and issuing death warrants . . ."

"Well, it's not that simple. True-true, you are HIV-positive. But it might take a while before the real illness . . . AIDS— you get from this bad blood—manifests itself. Having HIV is not the end of your life . . ."

"How long?"

"It could be a few months, it could be years . . . You see, this disease works like slow poison . . ."

"So it watches from the shadows of the bushes as its messengers eat you up, step by step, is that it?"

"Yes, something like that . . . When the time comes, you might begin to cough a lot. You might have big craw-craw all over your body. You will have diarrhoea. You will pass out a

lot of water and fluids from your body. Then your body will
begin to waste away because it is losing so much water, because of the slow poison in your body . . ."

Our neighbour broke down in the doctor's office and cried
and cried and cried. He came to the complete realisation of the
magnitude of this illness when the doctor referred him to the
Presbyterian Mission Hospital. The doctor asked him to come
and see Dr. Peter at your mission hospital. Our neighbour was
devastated. He came home a broken man. We couldn't believe
it when we heard the news. How does a father deal with such
news? It's always easier to deal with this illness when you
don't know the person. You hear someone has this disease and
you say, "oh!" or "sorry ooh" or "na which kana baluck dis
now?" and that's it. There is a safe distance between you and
that person. You express your sorrow because that's the right
thing to do and life goes on. But when you know someone, like
we knew our neighbour, someone for whose child we had all, at
one time of or another, given blood . . . when you know
someone that intimately, and you hear they have AIDS, you are
totally in shock. Shock. Pure and simple. You feel as if someone
has divulged a terrible secret that should have remained con-
cealed. You can't bear the weight of the bad news you are now
carrying. You know they've been sentenced to death. You
know they cannot reverse the verdict. You are conscious of
their certain death. You withdraw your tears. Your tears desert
you. Your tear glands dry up like the Sahara. You deny the illness, you banish it from your mind, but it won't leave. You
begin to have nightmares about it. You get angry. You want to
scream, you want to cry, but you can't. You think about the
meaning of the illness, the ramifications: is his wife infected?
What will happen to the children? You begin to think of them
as orphans—and that, while their father is still alive. But then,
that is nothing when you haven't come face to face with the
person. It is worse when you come face to face with someone

you know, someone you love who has AIDS. When I met my neighbour for the first time after that fateful trip to the hospital, I didn't even have the courage to extend my hand . . . I . . . I . . . I couldn't extend my hand. What's a greeting? Something we offer freely, everyday, to everybody—friends, family, and enemies alike. But there I was, standing in front of Pa Ambrose, and I couldn't offer my hand. I found it difficult to extend my hand. It seemed to weigh ten tons. It couldn't move. Later, only later, did I realise that I had unconsciously moved my hands towards my back. I had pretended to scratch my back. I had fidgeted with the ends of my wrappa and had pretended to wrap it more firmly round my waist. I had done everything so as not to offer my hand. I had even looked at the floor, searching my toes for jiggas that were not there. I couldn't look him straight in the eyes. This man, with whom I had joked and laughed so often in the past . . . this man, whose children have sat down and eaten food with me in my house . . . who call me mother. Our conversation was monosyllabic, monotonous: Hello. Hello. Morning. Morning. Bright day. Yes. Are these your eyes? Yes. Yours? Yes. How are you? Fine. How have you been? Sick. Your son? Fine. You see what I mean? A stupid conversation like that. Taking us nowhere. Although I was on my way to the market, I turned around and went back home. I remember thinking to myself on the way home: at least the child is safe, for now. Ambrose should count himself lucky. He will not be branded a wizard for eating his own son. What about mothers who kill the babies in their wombs with this disease without knowing it? Tegheh kwu! Ambrose is lucky indeed. He will be fine, I kept saying to myself. I didn't eat all day. I was so disgusted with myself. I was overwhelmed with sadness. I had never known such sadness. I had never known the day would come when I couldn't bring myself to greet my own neighbour, my own friend, my own blood. How do things like these happen? How?

It was about then that my son became the "fat virgin" man. Virgins and fat women seem to be in demand these days! Apparently, fat women do not have AIDS, or so Manoji claimed. He said fat women were less likely to have slow poison. I know our culture has always placed value on the shine of a woman's skin, on the plumpness of her curves, and especially on what these curves say about her husband's ability to take care of her, but this new craze about fat women and no AIDS was simply beyond me. Who can blame him or all the men who began to think like him? When people have AIDS, they lose weight so fast you can't even recognise someone you knew. They might have to call out to you and say, it's me, so so and so. Manoji was certain he had found the way to conquer this new ulcer that was quietly eating through the nervous system of our people. Then the time came and that fateful day came knocking on our door. My sister got ill and was wilting like a leaf in sun, before our eyes. I didn't believe the diviner who said her ex-husband was bewitching her. So I took her to the hospital to get her checked for worms. I knew it had to be worms or something easy to treat. They tested for worms. They said she had worms. But they also said she was anemic. They said she needed a blood transfusion, and only after that could she go home and pursue her treatment by eating a lot of vegetables and liver. Manoji offered to give his aunt the blood she needed. But first they had to pretest his blood. And the nurse said she had to tell us first why they had to test it.

"So you were given some pretest counselling by the hospital staff? That's good."

"Yes, even though I didn't see any need for the lecture."
Anyway, that woman reminded me that we should be grateful someone was taking the time to talk to us before taking our blood. She made it clear that pretest counselling for HIV wasn't done systematically in most hospitals. She told us that doctors had difficulty explaining to people why the blood they

were giving for relatives and friends had to be tested for AIDS. They had problems with donors who would refuse to give their blood for such a test or who would refuse to see or accept the results. She was relieved that wasn't the case with us. Manoji was prepared to do anything for his aunt, so he gave a blood sample and we waited. Waiting for the results was excruciating. Those six minutes we spent waiting for the rapid test are the longest six minutes I have ever spent in my entire life. Manoji, especially, made it feel like a lifetime. He paced up and down the hospital corridor. He bit on his nails. He stuck and removed his hands from his pockets more times than I could count. He was a nervous wreck. Anxiety was drumming tunes all over his face. The look in his eyes kept saying, What if? . . . what if I am? . . . what if I am HIV-positive? My worried look reflected back the same at him. What if the result is positive? we kept asking ourselves. The question kept pounding through my head. The feeling was op-pressive, overwhelming. The waiting was killing me. My palms were sweaty, my skin was aching. My blood pressure kept rising. My heart would not stop pounding. We were so nervous I wanted to open my mouth and scream, but my throat was completely dry. The wetness in my mouth seemed to have evaporated into thin air. Minutes felt like hours. You try to relax but you can't. You try to relax, you close your eyes but your eyelids are heavy and feel like rocks. Manoji paced up and down. Six minutes felt like six hours. Manoji paced up and down. Manoji bit on his nails. Six hours felt like six days. Manoji paced up and down. Manoji repeatedly stuck his hands in and out of his pockets. Six days felt like six years . . .

"Please sit down," the nurse said softly, almost too kindly. "I am sorry, I have bad news . . ."

" . . . "

"I am sorry to tell you that we cannot take your blood . . ."

" . . . "

"Mr. Manoji . . . you are HIV-positive, so we cannot collect your blood . . . we cannot give your blood to your aunt . . ."

" . . ."

"Please do not take this the wrong way. Being HIV-positive isn't the end of one's life, as most people think . . ."

" . . ."

"I understand how difficult this is, but . . . It's okay Mami. Hold him. Let him cry . . . it's alright."

"Sister, so what do we do now?" I heard a voice that sounded like mine ask the nurse.

Manoji's head was resting on my laps, his entire body convulsing as if fighting a bout of malaria fever, his hot tears leaving wet patches on my wrappa. I placed my hands on his shoulders, bent down, and rested my face on the back of his head. Our hearts were breaking like the sea waves that drenched our faces. After what seemed like an eternity, I felt the nurse's hand on my cheek, wiping away the tears.

"Mami Manoji, I am truly sorry . . . but I have to ask you . . . would you like me to test your blood . . . ?"

" . . ."

"Is it possible to ask someone else . . . another family member to give blood? . . ."

I have to tell you that in all this tragedy, what hurts most is what happens to families when a family member is HIV-positive or has AIDS—the breakdown of the family as we know it. I didn't mind the furtive looks, the whispering, the gossip, when it came from strangers, after all they didn't know me. They didn't know my son personally. I came to a point where I cared even less when people withdrew their hands in mid-air from a greeting or stepped back when it dawned on them my son had AIDS. I was only his caretaker . . . why wouldn't they shake my hand? Why wouldn't they hug me? They withdrew they hands, their smiles, their words, as if I were the plague. I erected a wall in my heart and shut out their callousness as we navigated from one hospital to the next, and between hospitals. I forgave them their ignorance. But how could I forgive my own family for slandering and deserting me and my son? They called my son a womaniser who had inherited his philandering ways from his mother. My son, a philanderer and I a prostitute! Imagine that. They all fled. The cowards. They deserted me. They were scared of me, as if I were a witch . . . as if I would curse them with slow poison and watch them die faster than my son. The cowards! They watched me from the bushes, as I shouldered his illness and his ailments; they watched as I cooked his food, cleaned his wounds, cleaned his body, removed the faeces from incessant diarrhoeal bouts that threatened everyday to kill him. I watched my son hurt as he coughed. I watched my son hurt as he drank water. I watched my son hurt as fluids drained out of his body like water disappearing in the sand. I watched my son waste away on the bed as friends and relatives stood safely in my nsaa and talked at me through the open door.

"Take him to the native doctor," they'd say. "I know so so and so. I hear he cures people who have slow poison in their blood. Take your son to him. He has a good reputation. He's the best in the land. Take your son to him. He'll cure your son . . ."

The hospitals had said over and over that there was no cure for AIDS and I had believed them, but when you have gone through what I have gone through, you begin to believe that they must be lying. You begin to say to yourself that there must be a treatment for the whiteman's slow poison, just as there is a treatment for our slow poison. At least with our slow poison, all you need is to know who cursed you in the first place, and that person can be persuaded to lift the curse and let you live. In the case of the whiteman's slow poison, you don't know who poisoned your blood, so how can your blood be treated? Some people even warned me that my son did not have the whiteman's slow poison but had been bewitched by one of my own relatives—my paternal granduncle, to be exact. Traditional medicine was the only cure my son needed, they insisted. Why was I wasting my time with whiteman medicine, they queried. I wanted the death of my son, they accused. Those frightened dogs, with their tails tucked between their legs, accused me of eating my own son! And without realising it, I was moving my son from one medicine man's compound to another.

"Did the native doctors help?"

"No."

"So you decided to come back home?"

"Yes. I came back because I couldn't afford it anymore. They had taken all I have: the litres of palmoil, the bundles of salt, the goats, the fowls, the money—those vultures! And they were killing my son with all sorts of concoctions that made him weaker day by day instead of purging and cleansing him of the poison, as they claimed. I had to come back. I came back because I wanted my son to die at home. To die at home with dignity. To die at home among his people, his ancestors. His people might have forsaken him but his ancestors would not. Never."

"I hear you."

"But I also came back home because I heard of your services. I heard about the charity work that the Presbyterian Mission was doing around the village for people who are dying from slow poison like my son . . . Sister, it is a great thing that your mission, your people are doing for us . . . It is a shame that your mission charity has taken on the responsibility of our government and our own families. Help, concern, kindness are things we do and offer each other because we're family. Now, other people . . . total strangers, have replaced our family . . . It's a terrible thing that's happening to us. This monster is threatening the very foundation on which our family institution is built. What are we going to do? What are we going to do . . . ?"

"Oh, Mami Manoji, I didn't know you still had tears in your eyes . . . Here, let me dry your face . . . You look like a little girl who's getting married when you cry like that . . ."

"Sister, you know I lost the desire to laugh. Why are you making me laugh? . . . I tell you, family is dead. Family isn't what it used to be. Not when it comes to AIDS. No, not when it comes to AIDS . . ."

" . . ."

"Can I ask you something, Sister?"

"Weh, Mami Manoji, you know you can ask me anything."

"Why doesn't your hospital keep people there, I mean, in the hospital itself?"

"It wasn't always like this. We used to hospitalise our AIDS patients. But as you know, ours is a small hospital and we don't have as many beds as we'd like to. Our AIDS patients used to take up beds . . ."

"So? I thought those beds are meant for patients."

"Yes, but they were taking up beds for months. Some, for long, long periods of time—years. And besides, they were . . ."

"Certain to die anyway . . ."

"Yes. We had to face the fact that they were all going to die and so instead of keeping the patients in the hospital, we decided to send them home. We created the association of nurses who would run an outreach program so that we could visit them weekly and provide them with care at home. Even though the hospital funds the outreach program, the program actually cuts costs . . ."

"Sister, I have to thank all of you. Everyday, I invoke the gods to come to our aid. I pray to the ancestors each night before I go to bed, that they bless us with more programs like yours. Your outreach program has done more for me than my own government, than my own family. Manoji and I both looked forward to the weekly visits your AIDS teams paid us. Your visits put a rare ray of hope and anticipation in our lives. We couldn't have survived without the drugs you provided weekly for his diarrhoea, the vitamins, the pain killers . . . We couldn't have survived it without the weekly counselling, the attention, the encouragement, the strength you gave us to move forward. Your visits were a moral booster that helped my son more than anything else. Those visits helped a mother deal with her grief. They helped my son and I watch him pass away in dignity. Sister, you should have seen him. When the time came, he wasn't afraid to go. He made peace with himself. He said good-bye in my arms . . . My son died. My son is dead, and still, I have to carry the stigma of what killed him like a badge. AIDS has claimed my son. AIDS has branded and banished me from my people. Do you know some fled before his body was even in the ground? They were disrespectful of their own blood. Fewer people attended and participated in the death celebrations. Death—life—we all celebrate; an event we all flock to, to cry, laugh, sing, dance, eat, and drink until we get drunk, whether we're connected by blood or not. They shunned him, even in death. Death! Life! . . . What kind of a disease is this that, like leprosy, is amputating our families, extremity by extremity, limb by limb? What kind of a disease is this that is taking away our words, cloaking us with silence, numbing us with fear? Eeh, Sister, you tell me."

Glossary

achu	Beba traditional food made of pounded tarot root
afofo	local gin; also known as arki, odontol, kembe fédéral
afuondo	all-powerful Beba medicine—afu means medicine, ndo means horn—a panacea, preserved in a small horn, usually given to people for protection of any kind and especially, from evil spirits and poison. If a child eats something that could be harmful to his/her health, the child is automatically given afuondo before any other treatment is administered
aki	mortar
asso	friend; also complice, kombi
Bakassi	Cameroonian peninsula, rich in oil, situated in the Gulf of Guinea. Also inhabited by Nigerians, this peninsula has been the source of bitter border conflicts between the two countries in recent years; also bakassi: slang for malaria
baluck	Pidgin, meaning bad luck; also badluck, for emphasis
banga	cannabis; also known as Indian hemp
bazin	West African cotton cloth used to make elaborately embroidered boubou for men and women
biebieh	Pidgin, meaning hair
biscuit bone	cartilage
bordel	brothel; Cameroonian usage: whore; also pute

boubou	traditional West African (wide) gown
CFA [franc]	Communauté Financière de l'Afrique. Currency used in former sub-Saharan French colonies. Also currently used in Equatorial Guinea (former Spanish colony) and Guinea Bissau (former Portuguese colony)
crish	Pidgin, meaning crazy; *also* cresh
Duala	language of the Douala people
DV	now in its sixth year (DV-2000), the "Diversity Immigrant Visa Program" is a visa lottery programme that grants persons from countries with lower immigration rates the opportunity to apply for one of 50,000 immigrant visas to the United States
eru	a vegetable with slightly tough leaves, harvested off vines, that grows in the forest
garri	West African staple food made from cassava; *also* tapioca
go-for-before-for-back	Pidgin, used to denote indecision or the attitude of someone wavering from one decision to another
groundnut	peanut
jigga	Pidgin, meaning chigger or chigoe
jigida	rows of brightly coloured small beads strung together, worn by young women around the waist
jobajo	another name for Beaufort, a lager beer brewed by the Brasseries du Cameroun
kaba ngondo	Douala traditional women's gown. Worn throughout Cameroon, it has been adopted as national attire
kanda	skin; *also*, edible cowhide used in making soups, obtained by either burning the hair off the skin or boiling the hide and cleaning off the hair with a knife
kombi	friend; *also* asso, complice
kpwefo	the most important, all-knowing Beba traditional regulatory society. The kpwefo holds the highest powers in the land. It assists the bezofo—the king makers—in crowning the new Fon. Made up of

	bekwop—nobles—this body holds in check the powers of the Fon and any other excesses of power. Although the bekwop assist the Fon in his decision making, the kpwefo can curb or veto some of their rash or radical decisions. The kpwefo also possesses medicinal powers that are the strongest in the land. Among its multiple duties, the kpwefo carries out the sanction of putting ngo'o on someone's chest (*see* ngo'o)
laterite	a reddish soil found in the humid tropics
Maggi cubes	chicken- or meat-flavoured bouillon cubes commonly used in soups
makossa	Douala traditional music and dance
mbenge	Duala, literally means "west," i.e., direction; commonly used to mean France, to denote Europe or the West
mbu'uh	palmwine, *also* mimbo
meker dze	small dried peas, brownish in colour
mimbo	generic term for alcoholic beverage; *see also* mbu'uh
ngo'o	literal: a very heavy stone; also used to refer to the ngbalii stone—basalt—used in making huge sculpture pieces for the Fon's palace.

figurative: when the Beba say, "the kpwefo has placed the ngo'o on someone's chest," it means the sanction of death—the ultimate punishment for unpardonable crimes—has been decreed for that person and is carried out by the kpwefo. In modern-day Beba, the sanction of death is sometimes replaced with banishment from the land, the culprit stripped of all titles and benefits of his clan. The compound and property of the exiled person revert to the Fon |
| njangi | a group or association of people who meet either weekly, bimonthly, or monthly to contribute money that is collected in turn by each of the members; and/or to save money that is shared among the members at the end of the year |

njagasa	traditional Beba skirt, quilt-like, made up of numerous long strips of pieces of different cloth, sewn together at the waistline only and worn by tying around the waist like a wrappa
nsaa	wide open space in a compound, located in front of a house(s) or in between houses, where children play. The nsaa is also used to conduct ceremonies, e.g., births, and for celebrations, e.g., deaths
ntip	Pidgin, meaning thief, *also* tif
off-licence	legally: a bar (sometimes doubling as a small goods store) or place where drinks are sold to be consumed elsewhere and supposed to close at 8 P.M. In reality, most of the drinks are consumed in the off-licence, which often stays open late into the night or closes only after the last customer leaves
okrika	secondhand clothing
pap	porridge made from cornmeal or millet, sweetened with sugar, sometimes flavored to taste with milk and/or freshly squeezed lemon juice
puff-puff	beignet
RCM	Roman Catholic Mission
sango	Duala, meaning Mister, Sir; man
so so and so	Pidgin, meaning so and so
tilly-lamp	a type of kerosene lamp that uses a thick wick and big glass globe. It shines brighter than a bush lamp, the glow sometimes maintained by pumping air into the kerosene tank
vono-bed	spring bed
wahala	trouble
wrappa	flowery cotton cloth, worn by wrapping around the waist

Monographs in International Studies

Titles Available from Ohio University Press

Southeast Asia Series

No. 56   Duiker, William J. Vietnam Since the Fall of Saigon. 1989. Updated ed. 401 pp. Paper 0-89680-162-4 $20.00.

No. 64   Dardjowidjojo, Soenjono. Vocabulary Building in Indonesian: An Advanced Reader. 1984. 664 pp. Paper 0-89680-118-7 $30.00.

No. 65   Errington, J. Joseph. Language and Social Change in Java: Linguistic Reflexes of Modernization in a Traditional Royal Polity. 1985. 210 pp. Paper 0-89680-120-9 $25.00.

No. 66   Binh, Tran Tu. The Red Earth: A Vietnamese Memoir of Life on a Colonial Rubber Plantation. Tr. by John Spragens. 1984. 102 pp. (SEAT*, V. 5) Paper 0-89680-119-5 $11.00.

No. 68   Syukri, Ibrahim. History of the Malay Kingdom of Patani. 1985. 135 pp. Paper 0-89680-123-3 $15.00.

No. 69   Keeler, Ward. Javanese: A Cultural Approach. 1984. 559 pp. Paper 0-89680-121-7 $25.00.

No. 70   Wilson, Constance M. and Lucien M. Hanks. Burma-Thailand Frontier Over Sixteen Decades: Three Descriptive Documents. 1985. 128 pp. Paper 0-89680-124-1 $11.00.

No. 71   Thomas, Lynn L. and Franz von Benda-Beckmann, eds. Change and Continuity in Minangkabau: Local, Regional, and Historical Perspectives on West Sumatra. 1985. 353 pp. Paper 0-89680-127-6 $16.00.

No. 72   Reid, Anthony and Oki Akira, eds. The Japanese Experience in Indonesia: Selected Memoirs of 1942–1945. 1986. 424 pp., 20 illus. (SEAT, V. 6) Paper 0-89680-132-2 $20.00.

* Southeast Asia Translation Project Group

No. 74   McArthur M. S. H. Report on Brunei in 1904. Introduced and Annotated by A. V. M. Horton. 1987. 297 pp. Paper 0-89680-135-7 $15.00.

No. 75   Lockard, Craig A. From Kampung to City: A Social History of Kuching, Malaysia, 1820–1970. 1987. 325 pp. Paper 0-89680-136-5 $20.00.

No. 76   McGinn, Richard, ed. Studies in Austronesian Linguistics. 1986. 516 pp. Paper 0-89680-137-3 $20.00.

No. 77   Muego, Benjamin N. Spectator Society: The Philippines Under Martial Rule. 1986. 232 pp. Paper 0-89680-138-1 $17.00.

No 79   Walton, Susan Pratt. Mode in Javanese Music. 1987. 278 pp. Paper 0-89680-144-6 $15.00.

No. 80   Nguyen Anh Tuan. South Vietnam: Trial and Experience. 1987. 477 pp., tables. Paper 0-89680-141-1 $18.00.

No. 82   Spores, John C. Running Amok: An Historical Inquiry. 1988. 190 pp. paper 0-89680-140-3 $13.00.

No. 83   Malaka, Tan. From Jail to Jail. Tr. by Helen Jarvis. 1911. 1209 pp., three volumes. (SEAT V. 8) Paper 0-89680-150-0 $55.00.

No. 84   Devas, Nick, with Brian Binder, Anne Booth, Kenneth Davey, and Roy Kelly. Financing Local Government in Indonesia. 1989. 360 pp. Paper 0-89680-153-5 $20.00.

No. 85   Suryadinata, Leo. Military Ascendancy and Political Culture: A Study of Indonesia's Golkar. 1989. 235 pp., illus., glossary, append., index, bibliog. Paper 0-89680-154-3 $18.00.

No. 86   Williams, Michael. Communism, Religion, and Revolt in Banten in the Early Twentieth Century. 1990. 390 pp. Paper 0-89680-155-1 $14.00.

No. 87   Hudak, Thomas. The Indigenization of Pali Meters in Thai Poetry. 1990. 247 pp. Paper 0-89680-159-4 $15.00.

No. 88   Lay, Ma Ma. Not Out of Hate: A Novel of Burma. Tr. by Margaret Aung-Thwin. Ed. by William Frederick. 1991. 260 pp. (SEAT V. 9) Paper 0-89680-167-5 $20.00.

No. 89   Anwar, Chairil. The Voice of the Night: Complete Poetry and Prose of Chairil Anwar. 1992. Revised Edition. Tr. by Burton Raffel. 196 pp. Paper 0-89680-170-5 $20.00.

No. 90   Hudak, Thomas John, tr., The Tale of Prince Samuttakote: A Buddhist Epic from Thailand. 1993. 230 pp. Paper 0-89680-174-8 $20.00.

No. 91 Roskies, D. M., ed. Text/Politics in Island Southeast Asia: Essays in Interpretation. 1993. 330 pp. Paper 0-89680-175-6 $25.00.

No. 92 Schenkhuizen, Marguérite, translated by Lizelot Stout van Balgooy. Memoirs of an Indo Woman: Twentieth-Century Life in the East Indies and Abroad. 1993. 312 pp. Paper 0-89680-178-0 $25.00.

No. 93 Salleh, Muhammad Haji. Beyond the Archipelago: Selected Poems. 1995. 247 pp. Paper 0-89680-181-0 $20.00.

No. 94 Federspiel, Howard M. A Dictionary of Indonesian Islam. 1995. 327 pp. Bibliog. Paper 0-89680-182-9 $25.00.

No. 95 Leary, John. Violence and the Dream People: The Orang Asli in the Malayan Emergency 1948–1960. 1995. 275 pp. Maps, illus., tables, appendices, bibliog., index. Paper 0-89680-186-1 $22.00.

No. 96 Lewis, Dianne. *Jan Compagnie* in the Straits of Malacca 1641–1795. 1995. 176 pp. Map, appendices, bibliog., index. Paper 0-89680-187-x. $18.00.

No. 97 Schiller, Jim and Martin-Schiller, Barbara. Imagining Indonesia: Cultural Politics and Political Culture. 1996. 384 pp., notes, glossary, bibliog. Paper 0-89680-190-x. $30.00.

No. 98 Bonga, Dieuwke Wendelaar. Eight Prison Camps: A Dutch Family in Japanese Java. 1996. 233 pp., illus., map, glossary. Paper 0-89680-191-8. $18.00.

No. 99 Gunn, Geoffrey C. Language, Ideology, and Power in Brunei Darussalam. 1996. 328 pp., glossary, notes, bibliog., index. Paper 0-86980-192-6 $24.00.

No. 100 Martin, Peter W., Conrad Ozog, and Gloria R. Poedjosoedarmo, eds. Language Use and Language Change in Brunei Darussalam. 1996. 390 pp., maps, notes, bibliog. Paper 0-89680-193-4 $26.00.

No. 101 Ooi, Keat Gin. Japanese Empire in the Tropics: Selected Documents and Reports of the Japanese Period in Sarawak, Northwest Borneo, 1941–1945. 1998. 740 pp., two volumes. Illus., maps, notes, index. Paper 0-89680-199-3 $50.00.

No. 102 Aung-Thwin, Michael A. Myth and History in the Historiography of Early Burma: Paradigms, Primary Sources, and Prejudices. 1998. 210 pp., maps, notes, bibliography, index. Paper 0-89680-201-9 $21.00.

No. 103 Pauka, Kirstin. Theater and Martial Arts in West Sumatra:

Randai and Silek of the Minang Kabou. 1999. 288 pp., illus., map, appendices, notes, bibliography, index. Paper 0-89680-205-1 $26.00.

Africa Series

No. 43   **Harik, Elsa M. and Donald G. Schilling.** The Politics of Education in Colonial Algeria and Kenya. 1984. 102 pp. Paper 0-89680-117-9 $12.50.

No. 45   **Keto, C. Tsehloane.** American-South African Relations 1784–1980: Review and Select Bibliography. 1985. 169 pp. Paper 0-89680-128-4 $11.00.

No. 46   **Burness, Don,** ed. Wanasema: Conversations with African Writers. 1985. 103 pp. paper 0-89680-129-2 $11.00.

No. 47   **Switzer, Les.** Media and Dependency in South Africa: A Case Study of the Press and the Ciskei "Homeland." 1985. 97 pp. Paper 0-89680-130-6 $10.00.

No. 51   **Clayton, Anthony and David Killingray.** Khaki and Blue: Military and Police in British Colonial Africa. 1989. 347 pp. Paper 0-89680-147-0 $20.00.

No. 52   **Northrup, David.** Beyond the Bend in the River: African Labor in Eastern Zaire, 1865–1940. 1988. 282 pp. Paper 0-89680-151-9 $15.00.

No. 53   **Makinde, M. Akin.** African Philosophy, Culture, and Traditional Medicine. 1988. 172 pp. Paper 0-89680-152-7 $16.00.

No. 54   **Parson, Jack,** ed. Succession to High Office in Botswana: Three Case Studies. 1990. 455 pp. Paper 0-89680-157-8 $20.00.

No. 56   **Staudinger, Paul.** In the Heart of the Hausa States. Tr. by Johanna E. Moody. Foreword by Paul Lovejoy. 1990. In two volumes., 469 + 224 pp., maps, apps. Paper 0-89680-160-8 (2 vols.) $35.00.

No. 57   **Sikainga, Ahmad Alawad.** The Western Bahr Al-Ghazal under British Rule, 1898–1956. 1991. 195 pp. Paper 0-89680-161-6 $15.00.

No. 58   **Wilson, Louis E.** The Krobo People of Ghana to 1892: A Political and Social History. 1991. 285 pp. Paper 0-89680-164-0 $20.00.

No. 59   **du Toit, Brian M.** Cannabis, Alcohol, and the South African

Student: Adolescent Drug Use, 1974–1985. 1991. 176 pp., notes, tables. Paper 0-89680-166-7 $17.00.

No. 60   Falola, Toyin and Dennis Itavyar, eds. The Political Economy of Health in Africa. 1992. 258 pp., notes, tables. Paper 0-89680-166-7 $20.00.

No. 61   Kiros, Tedros. Moral Philosophy and Development: The Human Condition in Africa. 1992. 199 pp., notes. Paper 0-89680-171-3 $20.00.

No. 62   Burness, Don. Echoes of the Sunbird: An Anthology of Contemporary African Poetry. 1993. 198 pp. Paper 0-89680-173-x $17.00.

No. 64   Nelson, Samuel H. Colonialism in the Congo Basin 1880–1940. 1994. 290 pp. Index. Paper 0-89680-180-2 $23.00.

No. 66   Ilesanmi, Simeon Olusegun. Religious Pluralism and the Nigerian State. 1996. 336 pp., maps, notes, bibliog., index. Paper 0-89680-194-2 $23.00.

No. 67   Steeves, H. Leslie. Gender Violence and the Press: The St. Kizito Story. 1997. 176 pp., illus., notes, bibliog., index. Paper 0-89680195-0 $17.95.

No. 68   Munro, William A. The Moral Economy of the State: Conservation, Community Development, and State-Making in Zimbabwe. 1998. 510 pp., maps, notes, bibliog., index. Paper 0-89680-202-7 $26.00.

No. 69   Rubert, Steven C. A Most Promising Weed: A History of Tobacco Farming and Labor in Colonial Zimbabwe, 1890–1945. 1998. 264 pp., illus., maps, notes, bibliog., index. Paper 0-89680-203-5 $26.00.

Latin America Series

No. 9   Tata, Robert J. Structural Changes in Puerto Rico's Economy: 1947–1976. 1981. 118 pp. Paper 0-89680-107-1 $12.00.

No. 13   Henderson, James D. Conservative Thought in Latin America: The Ideas of Laureano Gomez. 1988. 229 pp. Paper 0-89680-148-9 $16.00.

No. 17   Mijeski, Kenneth J., ed. The Nicaraguan Constitution of 1987: English Translation and Commentary. 1991. 355 pp. Paper 0-89680-165-9 $25.00.

No. 18   Finnegan, Pamela. The Tension of Paradox: José Donoso's

The Obscene Bird of Night as Spiritual Exercises. 1992. 204 pp. Paper 0-89680-169-1 $15.00.

No. 19   Kim, Sung Ho and Thomas W. Walker, eds. Perspectives on War and Peace in Central America. 1992. 155 pp., notes, bibliog. Paper 0-89680-172-1 $17.00.

No. 20   Becker, Marc. Mariátegui and Latin American Marxist Theory. 1993. 239 pp. Paper 0-89680-177-2 $20.00.

No. 21   Boschetto-Sandoval, Sandra M. and Marcia Phillips McGowan, eds. Claribel Alegría and Central American Literature. 1994. 233 pp., illus. Paper 0-89680-179-9 $20.00.

No. 22   Zimmerman, Marc. Literature and Resistance in Guatemala: Textual Modes and Cultural Politics from El Señor Presidente to Rigoberta Menchú. 1995. 2 volume set 320 + 370 pp., notes, bibliog. Paper 0-89680-183-7 $50.00.

No. 23   Hey, Jeanne A. K. Theories of Dependent Foreign Policy: The Case of Ecuador in the 1980s. 1995. 280 pp., map, tables, notes, bibliog., index. Paper 0-89680-184-5 $22.00.

No. 24   Wright, Bruce E. Theory in the Practice of the Nicaraguan Revolution. 1995. 320 pp., notes, illus., bibliog., index. Paper 0-89680-185-3. $23.00.

No. 25   Mann, Carlos Guevara. Panamanian Militarism: A Historical Interpretation. 1996. 243 pp., illus., map, notes, bibliog., index. Paper 0-89680-189-6 $23.00.

No. 26   Armony, Ariel. Argentina, the United States, and the Anti-Communist Crusade in Central America. 1997. 305 pp. (est.) illus., maps, notes, bibliog., index. Paper 0-89680-196-9 $26.00.

No. 27   Sandoval, Ciro A. and Sandra M. Boschetto-Sandoval, eds. José María Arguedas: Reconsiderations for Latin American Studies. 1998. 350 pp., notes, bibliog. Paper 0-89680-200-0 $23.00.

No. 28   Zimmerman, Marc and Raúl Rojas, eds. Voices From the Silence: Guatemalan Literature of Resistance. 1998. 572 pp., bibliog., index. Paper 0-89680-198-5 $23.00.

Ordering Information

Individuals are encouraged to patronize local bookstores wherever possible. Orders for titles in the Monographs in International Studies may be placed directly through the Ohio University Press, Scott Quadrangle, Athens, Ohio 45701-2979. Individuals should remit payment by check,

VISA, or MasterCard.* Those ordering from the United Kingdom, Continental Europe, the Middle East, and Africa should order through Academic and University Publishers Group, 1 Gower Street, London WC1E, England. Orders from the Pacific Region, Asia, Australia, and New Zealand should be sent to East-West Export Books, c/o the University of Hawaii Press, 2840 Kolowalu Street, Honolulu, Hawaii 96822, USA.

Individuals ordering from outside of the U.S. should remit in U.S. funds to Ohio University Press either by International Money Order or by a check drawn on a U.S. bank.** Most out-of-print titles may be ordered from University Microfilms, Inc., 300 North Zeeb Road, Ann Arbor, Michigan 48106, USA.

Prices are subject to change.

Ohio University
Center for International Studies

The Ohio University Center for International Studies was established to help create within the university and local communities a greater awareness of the world beyond the United States. Comprising programs in African, Latin American, Southeast Asian, Development and Administrative studies, the Center supports scholarly research, sponsors lectures and colloquia, encourages course development within the university curriculum, and publishes the Monographs in International Studies series with the Ohio University Press. The Center and its programs also offer an interdisciplinary Master of Arts degree in which students may focus on one of the regional or topical concentrations, and may also combine academics with training in career fields such as journalism, business, and language teaching. For undergraduates, major and certificate programs are also available.

For more information, contact the Vice Provost for International Studies, Burson House, Ohio University, Athens, Ohio 45701.